To Madison Teresa Geering

With all my love, Nana Faeries

And with thanks to ….

Jim Empett the best 'boss' anyone could have. Thank you for your support, and yes another one for you to buy.

Neil Minter for believing in my writing ability, and thanks for that yummy alfresco meal last summer. What a night.

All my writing friends at Night Publishing, who are oh so supportive.

Tim Roux Managing Editor at Night Publishing. Where would any of us be without you honey.

My family - you inspire me to keep on writing.

Shasta Summer

by

Teresa Geering

Part of the 'Erasmus, Shasta & Merlin' series

ISBN   1463574185

EAN   978-1463574185

'Shasta Summer' is published by Night Publishing which can be contacted at: http://www.nightpublishing.com.

'Shasta Summer' forms part of the romance / fantasy series 'Erasmus, Shasta & Merlin' which includes the previously released 'The Eye of Erasmus'.

Book 1:

The Enchanted Garden

Chapter 1

How many of us are given the chance to relive our past lives? Indeed, would we want to?

Summer Backer was given just that opportunity.

Born to Iris and George Backer eight years previously, an only child with bright red hair, she typically burned in the sun without factor fifty. There was a strong bond between Summer and her parents. This will hold good through her current life, and when she is required to visit her past life.

The Backers owned a large rambling, five bedroomed property. A long stony drive led up to the front of the house, with beds of roses growing to the side. The back garden went on indefinitely, with neat orderly flowerbeds and a few popular trees planted here and there. Giles, the gardener, did all the heavy work, while Iris pottered around with her wooden trug picking flowers for the house.

George owned two garden centres, one locally and the other in Holland. Each spring and autumn he took a trip over to Holland to see his manager, Henney, who ran the Dutch centre. All other business was dealt with by phone.

The family's lifestyle was completely idyllic and this summer was going to be no different except ....

* * *

It was the beginning of the summer holidays, and Summer was lying in the garden under the willow tree watching her mother pick flowers for the entrance hall of the house. A bee was buzzing close by collecting pollen and making her feel very sleepy. She rolled over onto her back and looked up at the sun through the branches of the tree. Mentally she started planning her sleepover that night with Holly, her closest school friend. In the distance she could hear the telephone ringing. Moments later her father came into the garden and was deep in conversation with her mother.

"But, George, what will we do with Summer?" asked her mother in a raised voice, completely out of character.

"Couldn't she stay with your sister, May, in Shasta?" asked her father.

"I suppose so, but May is so eccentric," her mother replied distractedly.

Summer's curiosity got the better of her and, as she started to get up, her mother called out to her.

"Summer, will you come here, please?"

"Coming. What's happened?"

"Your father has had a phone call from Henney. There is a problem with some of this year's plants and we have to go over."

Summer knew if her mother was going, it meant BIG trouble.

"I'll give my sister, May, a ring. Perhaps you can stay with her at the cottage in Shasta. It might be a bit boring for you but I don't see what else we can do. Holland will be even more boring for you."

"Do I have to go? Couldn't I stay with Holly instead? I'm going to miss my sleepover and I don't know Aunt May very well."

"I'm sorry, Summer, not this time. We don't know how long we'll be away yet. We can't expect your friends' parents to look after you at such short notice," her mother said.

With that, her mother went into the house and phoned her aunt. Summer had no choice - she was going. Aunt May would be delighted to have the company, apparently. The last time she had seen Summer was when she was still very small. At that time she had given her a doll that she had made herself. It was stuffed with cotton wool and had long blonde plaits made out of pale yellow wool and dungarees. When she got home she sat her on her bed and decided to call her Primrose. She usually took her with her when she stayed overnight with friends.

Her mother didn't visit her sister very often because she lived some distance away, but they spoke on the telephone on a regular basis. As Summer didn't remember her, she had no idea what to expect, and what did 'eccentric' mean, she wondered.

Holly's parents were informed of the change in plans and a promise of a double sleepover was made once she returned, to make up for it. The rest of the day was spent packing suitcases. Time was of the essence and her mother was not only supervising her case but ensuring that her father had enough of everything. Her parents intended to drop her off at aunt May's cottage, then get the ferry from Dover to Calais and drive on to Holland from there. With delicate care, Summer lifted Primrose off the bed and decided to carry her instead of packing her in the suitcase. She was getting a bit ragged now as Summer used to suck on her foot when she was small, but she still loved her dearly.

The following morning it started to rain just as they were leaving. There wasn't much traffic, so they reached the outskirts of the village by 11 o'clock. As they drove into Shasta, the rain suddenly stopped and Summer saw a rainbow in the distance which appeared to end in the garden of a cottage.

"How strange," said her mother, "the rainbow seems to stop in May's garden."

Summer began to feel unexpected excitement all of a sudden.

Chapter 2

They parked outside the cottage and, while her father was unloading her suitcases, she and her mother approached the wooden gate which formed part of a trellis archway. An abundance of red and white roses climbed from ground level to meet at the top of the trellis. The perfume was much stronger than their own roses at home. Walking through the arch and down the path, they passed many flowers on the way, all different varieties, some of which Summer recognised but she couldn't remember their names. Nothing was in straight lines like their borders at home; the flowers just seemed to grow where they took a fancy. Above the door hung a wooden nameplate but Summer wasn't tall enough to read it. Her mother lifted the knocker to announce their arrival and it came away in her hand.

With an exaggerated sigh she laid it on the ground. "Typical of May," she muttered.

"What do you mean, Mum?" Summer asked.

Still carrying on talking as if she hadn't heard her, her mother said, "When will she get that fixed properly? The same thing happened at the last visit. Your aunt will always be a bit eccentric, I think".

There was that word again. As Summer was about to ask what it meant, the door was opened wide. A tall, thin woman, who looked a bit like a traditional gypsy, stood framed in the doorway. She was wearing a long flowing, very low cut dress that reached to her ankles. It was the type of dress Summer's mother would refer to as "quite disgusting". On both her wrists were endless silver bracelets that seemed to jangle with every movement. Her black hair was in one long plait which hung over her right shoulder. Summer was amazed to see it reached down to her waist. The end of the plait was tied in multi-coloured ribbons. Although she was older than

Summer's mother, she seemed to have a much younger face.

"Hello, May" said her mother, "lovely to see you again," and kissed her on the cheek.

Aunt May returned the kiss and bent down to give Summer a hug. As she put her arms around her neck, Summer could smell her perfume which reminded her of the roses. Her bracelets rattled together and her bright brown eyes seemed to crinkle up into a smile.

"Hello, my lovely, you and I are going to have such a wonderful time together. I see you still have Primrose, then".

"How did you know she was called Primrose, Aunt May, and why are you eccentric?" Summer asked.

"Summer, don't be so rude!!" her mother exclaimed in embarrassment.

Aunt May just smiled, put her arm around her and took her inside the cottage.

"Come, my lovely, let's get you settled in. First, though, I think a nice cool drink is called for, then I will show you to your room when your parents leave."

Her father, having caught them up, put Summer's suitcases just inside the door, called out "Hello" to Aunt May, and walked with her mother and her through the kitchen into the garden. Summer noticed a black cat curled up in a large wicker chair in the kitchen. He was stretched out on patchwork cushions. As she passed, it opened its eyes and looked straight at her. Satisfied that she wasn't going to disturb him, he yawned and went back to sleep. Summer's parents were already sitting down at a rustic table with four chairs around it. Summer sat in the swing seat which had just enough room for two. Aunt May came out carrying a tray with four tall glasses containing a yellow coloured drink that Summer didn't recognise. She set the tray down on the table and brought Summer's drink over to her.

"What's this drink called, Aunt?" Summer asked.

"Why, it's lemonade dear," she said surprised.

"Our lemonade at home isn't anything like this. It hasn't got any colour really, and it's fizzy,"

"Ah, this is home made. I'll show you how to make it, if you like".

"Yes, please," Summer said.

Suddenly Summer started to yawn. She had slept most of the journey, so why was she tired again so soon? Having finished their drinks, her parents decided to start their journey towards Dover. Kissing her goodbye affectionately, her mother yet again gave her the usual lecture about behaving herself and promised she would write newsy letters to her or phone from Holland. Her father gave her a kiss and a hug, and said while she was here maybe she could help her aunt with her garden; it would give her an opportunity to learn some of the names of the flowers. With an exaggerated wink at her aunt, he made his way to the car. Waving goodbye to her parents as the car turned the corner, Summer turned and saw that her aunt was making her way back down the path towards the cottage. Summer suddenly realised that she was muttering to the plants as she went past. When they reached the front door, she picked up the door knocker from where her mother had laid it and hung it back on the door again. Somehow it just stayed there, waiting to be used by the next caller.

"Will you tell me the name of the cottage, please, Aunt. I'm not tall enough to read the name?"

"Oh, it used to be called Primrose Cottage because there are lots of evening primroses growing here. I changed it to Rainbow's End, though, because the rainbows always seem to end at the bottom of the garden by Faery Cove," she replied.

"Faery Cove?!!" Summer gasped.

"Oh yes. Didn't I tell you I had faeries at the bottom of my garden, child?" she replied in a matter-of-fact way.

As Summer looked at her in disbelief, she started to yawn again.

"I think I'll show you to your room and you can have a nap. The journey must have tired you."

Aunt May picked up her two cases and showed Summer to her bedroom which was next to Aunt May's. To the side was a small bathroom. The only other rooms in the cottage were the sitting room and the kitchen which had a large wooden table in the middle with several chairs around it.

Summer's bedroom was smaller than at home. There was a double bed with a patchwork cover on it which matched the curtains. On either side of the bed was a chest of drawers, and in the far corner a wardrobe. In the other corner was another wicker chair with lots more patchwork cushions. This was similar to the one in the kitchen that the cat was sleeping on.

Summer also noticed that the ceilings seemed to slant down and meet the walls at strange angles. It wouldn't do to be too tall as you would have to duck all the time.

"Why don't you lie down on the bed and have a bit of a sleep, Summer? It will make you feel much better."

As Aunt May pulled back the patchwork cover, Summer took off her shoes and curled up on the bed with Primrose. She seemed to snuggle down into it and it was so much more comfy than her bed at home. Aunt May pulled the cover back over her and drew the curtains together. Leaving the door ajar, she left the room.

* * *

As Summer started to drift into sleep, she remembered that her aunt had known the name of her doll without asking, It was also strange that the name of the cottage had been Primrose Cottage as well. Were there really faeries at the bottom of the garden, she wondered. Her mother always insisted she put her baby teeth under the pillow for the tooth faery. In the morning they had always disappeared and coins were left in their place. She was nearly nine now, though, and far too old to believe in them. Wasn't she? All

13

these thoughts passed through her head as she slowly drifted into a deep sleep.

While Summer was asleep, her aunt came back into the bedroom. Very quietly she set about unpacking the cases. She hung some of her niece's things in the wardrobe and put other bits in the chests of drawers. The cat padded into the room and jumped onto the wicker chair watching.

In hushed tones her aunt said, "Hasn't she grown into a lovely girl, Merlin? We will have to do something about that red hair, though. Even with sun cream and a hat she will burn in our garden."

Equally quietly Merlin agreed. "Maybe we could turn it blonde in time for Shasta Day. By the way, are you using my earthly name of Snoops while she's here, May? And have you decided to tell her that I can talk? I get a bit fed up having to pretend with miaow this and that."

"I don't know yet, Merlin. She's only eight, so perhaps we had better wait awhile until she has met Abelia, the faery queen. In the meantime I think we will call you Snoops and don't get grumpy because you have to act like a cat," May replied.

"I've been a cat for so many years now, when do you think I will turn back into human form again?" Merlin asked.

"Maybe quite soon, Merlin," she said.

"Perhaps we should ask the Book of Erasmus later this evening."

With that, May walked silently out of the room followed by Merlin.

14

Chapter 3

Summer woke up the following morning unsure where she was at first. Although the curtains were drawn, the room was very bright which hinted at a sunny morning. She also noticed that she was completely under all the covers and was wearing her nightdress. Her aunt must have undressed her while she was asleep and, boy, was she hungry now. Summer could smell coffee which was at least a familiar smell to her. Father drank endless cups of coffee every morning. Her mother had tea, always made in a pot with traditional tea leaves.

Stretching her arms up over her head, she climbed out of bed, slipped her feet into her slippers, and put on her dressing gown which had been laid on the bottom of the bed. As she walked over to the window to pull the curtains back, she was startled to see that the cat was curled up on the wicker chair watching her. Should she stroke it, she wondered. She took a chance and rested her hand on its head. With a quiet miaow, the cat, uncomplaining, uncurled its body and began to stretch. While Summer pulled the curtains back to let in the sun, the cat jumped down and waited for her, then walked out beside her into the kitchen. Her aunt was sitting at the kitchen table drinking coffee.

"Good morning, my lovely, did you sleep well?" she asked in that lovely flowing voice.

"Yes, thank you, Aunt May. I must have been very tired to sleep for so long".

"People often say that when they visit this village, child. Sit down at the table and I will get you a drink and some breakfast. You must be very hungry this morning." Summer agreed she was starving.

"Later on, we can take a walk through the village and buy some more provisions. I didn't have much time to ask your mother what your likes and dislikes are. Now, what would you like for breakfast,

Summer? I have cereal with eggs and toast. Will that be alright?"

"Cereal and some orange juice, if you have any please, Aunty."

Aunt May put the cereal packet, bowl and jug of milk in front of Summer, telling her to help herself.

"I'll just get the juice from the fridge. The spoons are in the cutlery drawer of the dresser."

Summer helped herself to cereal and milk, and used the teaspoon in the sugar bowl to sprinkle on sugar. Rising to get a spoon from the dresser, she heard her aunt talking to herself as she bent over the fridge. There seemed very little of anything in there as far as Summer could see, and certainly no orange juice. As she returned to the table, she heard the fridge door close. As she sat down, her aunt came towards her with a glass of fresh juice. Summer couldn't believe her eyes. Her face must have shown her disbelief because her aunt asked, "Is anything the matter, child?"

"Oh... Err... no Aunt, thank you," she said as she accepted the juice.

The cat walked to and fro in front of May, rubbing his back up against her legs.

"Yes, yes, I haven't forgotten you. Maybe some tinned tuna fish this morning."

Hearing this, the cat began to miaow continuously.

Having recovered from her surprise over the juice, Summer asked, "Is the cat a boy or a girl, and what is it called?"

"It's a male cat and his name is Snoops because he is always snooping around."

Hearing that, Merlin twitched his tail, stuck his head in the air and walked over to the wicker chair. Jumping up, he circled the cushions a couple of times and then lay down. As May put his breakfast dish on to the floor, he jumped down again and ran over to it. Pouring herself another cup of coffee, May came and sat at the table with Summer.

"When you've finished your breakfast, Summer, I'll wash and dry

16

the dishes, if you will make your bed for me, please. Then we can take that walk down to the village."

"Yes, please, Aunt. That would be lovely."

"I'm really going to enjoy having you here to stay, Summer. You'll be company for Snoops and me. I hope you won't be too bored".

"I'm sure I won't be, Aunt," and she realised she meant it.

Leaving her aunt to wash the dishes, she went into her bedroom to make her bed.

As she passed her aunt's bedroom, the door was open and she couldn't resist looking inside. It was almost identical to her room, except the colours were different, brighter somehow. Taking a chance, Summer peered round behind the door. There was an altar with a white cloth covering it, a bit like in the churches. In a vase were fresh flowers of all kinds, but mostly deep red in colour. In the middle of the altar was a dark green scarf with several brown leaves, twigs and stones, also a rather large brown book on which was written in gold 'The Eye of Erasmus'. She was tempted to touch it, but something held her back. *No, not now*, she thought. To one side were several candles in different colours. At either end of the altar were two brass candlesticks with a brown candle in each that had been used. Also there was a lovely smell about the room which reminded her of the garden.

Suddenly realising that she was trespassing, she backed out of the room and trod on the cat which let out a horrible screech. Bending down, she stroked him and he began to purr. Telling him she was sorry, she made her way to her bedroom.

The cat jumped up and sat in the middle of the bed.

"Snoops, I can't make the bed if you are sitting in the middle. Will you get off please?"

The cat, obviously deciding to play, stretched himself to his full length and just lay there. Summer laughed and tickled his tummy which made him purr even more.

"SNOOPS get off the bed, please, and let Summer make it."

He complained, but duly jumped off and went out towards the kitchen in disgust.

Summer hadn't heard her aunt come up behind her and it made her jump.

"I'm sorry to have made you jump, but that cat thinks he owns the cottage sometimes. Here, let me go on the other side and we'll make the bed between us."

Once the bed was made and the windows were opened to air the room, Aunt May collected an oblong wicker basket from the kitchen and they made their way into the village. As they walked up the path, Summer's aunt bent down to cup several flowers under the petals, praising them for their beauty.

"Do you talk to all your plants, Aunt May?"

"Yes, of course. They like to be told how pretty they are. They will reward you by growing even more beautiful."

"I never thought of that," Summer said.

Although Summer had her own little garden at home, she only weeded round the flowers when she felt like it, giving it a bit of a dig with a trowel. Giles, the gardener, always did any heavy work.

"There's so much I need to learn about growing flowers, Aunt. My father was right. Can I help you with your garden and perhaps you will help me to learn about the different flowers?"

"It will be my pleasure, Summer. If it isn't too hot after lunch we will make a start then."

As they started off down the road, Summer started to get that excited feeling back again. Things were going really well. There was no reason for her to feel bored at all.

Walking through the village, many people stopped to say hello, and each time Aunt May introduced Summer. Sometimes people would just call from the other side of the road, saying things like, "Hello, May. My back is much better now, thanks to your potion", or "My sore throat has gone, May. The herbs really worked".

"What are they talking about, Aunt May, and what is a potion?"

"Hush, child, I'll explain when we get home. Now let's go into this shop and get some shopping."

"Aren't we going to the supermarket, Aunt?"

Aunt May started to laugh, which sounded just like bells tinkling. "Goodness no, my lovely, we don't have a supermarket here in Shasta. Anything we want we can buy in this shop."

As Summer pushed open the door, her aunt followed her in. It seemed very dark at first but, after a while, Summer's eyes adjusted. On one long counter were many jars of all sorts of different jams and marmalades. Standing in two of the corners were bran tubs. On closer inspection, Summer noted that they contained mostly tins of fruit. They were cushioned on layers of sawdust, presumably to stop them getting dented. They reminded Summer of a lucky dip where it was pot luck as to what you pulled out. Not a problem, she supposed, if you had plenty of time to spare. Along the wall were tall freezers with frozen goods. So, no, she supposed the village didn't really need a supermarket.

Having decided what they wanted, Aunt May packed the goods in her basket, paid the shopkeeper and they were out in the bright sunshine again. Summer suddenly realised she had forgotten to put any sun cream on her skin and her arms were starting to go a bit red. Summer was sure her nose would be burnt too.

"Shall we get a cool drink, Summer, before we start back?"

"Oh, yes please, Aunt. That would be nice."

"Come on, then," she said. "Let's go over there in the shade."

It was a bit like the teashops Summer had visited with her parents whilst on holiday in Devon. While her aunt went inside to get their drinks, Summer sat down at a table set under a tree. As she looked around towards the village green opposite, she suddenly had a mental picture of people dancing to music. They weren't dressed in the current fashion, more like you saw in the history books in the library at school. How very odd, thought Summer, as the image vanished just as quickly as it had appeared. She wondered what people did here in the summer and why there weren't many children either.

Aunt May came out carrying two glasses of orange juice which had ice cubes floating in the top.

"Thank you, Aunt. I haven't noticed many children here. Where are they all?"

"Quite a few of the village children go away to school and they don't finish for another week yet."

"Oh, I see," said Summer.

"Next week the village celebrates Shasta Day. All the people of the village get together on the green. We have music with Morris dancers, food and drink, and just enjoy ourselves. Very soon the villagers will start putting up the maypole again, but this time they will choose a Shasta Queen instead of a May Queen.

"Why is it called Shasta Day, Aunt?"

"Well, my lovely, Shasta was a travelling woman who lived many years ago. She would turn up in a village, spend some time there, and then move on. When she arrived here it wasn't a very welcoming place. The people were a bit frightened of her because she had very long blonde hair which was worn in a plait like mine. Blonde hair was unusual then, as nearly everyone had brown or black hair. Mostly they just kept their distance from her. As she travelled through the village, everywhere she went there seemed to be weeds growing. The flowers had all died. One day she went into the back of her caravan, which was painted in beautiful rich colours, and brought out a large black cooking pot with three legs. Curiosity got the better of the villagers and they started to gather round to see what she was doing. Inside the pot she placed a selection of herbs and seed pods that looked very dried up. Then, gathering up a few twigs, she lit a small fire underneath the pot. After a while, a very strange but pleasant smell came from the pot and it seemed to have a hypnotic effect on the villagers. Nodding their head in approval, they were happy just to sit in silence watching. Suddenly,

Shasta began to hum quietly to herself whilst stirring the contents of the pot with a stick which had been lying nearby. One by one the villagers joined in the humming and took it in turns to stir the pot. Eventually, as the night sky began to lighten into a new dawn, Shasta held up her hand for silence.

'"My friends," she said, "each of you will take one seed pod from the pot. When you open it, you will see inside two seeds. You must plant one seed in the hedgerow and one seed in your garden. Each seed will be different. This should be done at sunset tonight."

"So each villager did as she asked. The following morning, in each garden and every hedgerow, a new flower had grown where each weed had been. The villagers were so happy to see so many pretty flowers, they asked Shasta to stay in the village and named it after her. In celebration, they all gathered on the green that night. All the women and maidens wore garlands of flowers with leaves in their hair and danced with the men and boys. Ale flowed freely and they talked and danced from sunset until the following morning."

"What a lovely story, Aunt."

"And that is why so many Shasta daisies grow in the village. Those are Shasta daisies there, my child, and there and there. Now let's get back with the shopping and see what Snoops has been up to."

With the shopping put away, Aunt May offered to show Summer how to make lemonade, which turned out to be very easy. It was just the juice of fresh lemons, some sugar, mint from the garden, then with one secret ingredient added. Usually Summer would have insisted on knowing what the secret ingredient was but, here in the village, it didn't seem to matter very much. Summer was learning to accept whatever her aunt told her without asking too many questions. Summer was then given a choice of spending the afternoon lazing in the garden or of walking around with her Aunt and learning some of the plants' names. She decided to laze in the garden.

"Very well, Summer, on condition that you wear your sun hat and lots of sun cream."

"Ok, Aunt," she said.

Although her aunt's garden was much disorganised, it had lots of trees and bushes that provided shade. Summer chose to sit under one of the trees. As she lay on her back, she started to doze. Suddenly she heard voices coming from behind the honeysuckle bush. She recognised her aunt's voice, but there was also a male voice that she didn't recognise. Had she got a visitor, she wondered?

The voice was speaking again now.

"Unless we do something about her red hair, May, Summer will keep burning in the sun."

"I agree," said her aunt.

Curiosity finally got the better of her, and Summer edged closer to the honeysuckle bush. Making a small opening between the leaves, she peered through. She could only see her aunt and Snoops, so to whom was she talking?

"I think the best thing is for us to suggest we change it to blonde for Shasta Day, Merlin. After all, she will be the Shasta Queen."

"Right," said Merlin.

Summer sat back on her heels and thought about what she had just seen and heard. She was eight and three quarters, which meant nearly nine. That was nearly grown up, and the following year she would be in double figures. Her mother always told everyone. "Summer is a very sensible child with a screwed on head."

But she had just witnessed a cat talking. Summer knew she hadn't imagined it.

Summer was bubbling with excitement. Imagine being able to talk with a cat, and why had Aunt called him Merlin? Why was she going to be the Shasta Queen, and how did they know that? So many questions...

As Summer crept forward, her aunt and the cat rose to go in. She followed them at a distance. Her aunt was standing by the back door and Snoops was curled up in the swing seat.

"Hello, Summer," she said. "Did you have a nice sleep in the garden?"

"Yes, thank you. Well no, not really. I thought I heard Snoops talking to you.".

"Well, yes, of course he does. In fact all cats talk to their keepers."

"But I mean talking in a human voice," Summer replied.

"Oh, I see," said Aunt May.

Scooping Snoops up in her arms, she sat on the swing seat and patted the space beside her for Summer to sit with her. As Summer sat down, she began stroking the cat in a gentle rhythm.

"Well, child, I see you have discovered our secret, so I had better tell you the story. Many years ago, Merlin - yes that is his real name – was a young boy about your age. He was trying out different spells with his master and, by accident, he was turned into a cat. Try as he might, his master couldn't find a spell to reverse it. So, ever since then, he has had to live life as a cat. He has used up his nine lives many times and lived with many families through the ages, so when I came home one day and he was sitting on my doorstep, I invited him to live with me. When he felt he could trust me, he told me his story. I feel very privileged to have him living with me now. As you are also very special, Summer, we are now entrusting you with our secret."

"Thank goodness," said Merlin, "now I won't have to do any more of that silly meowing any more."

With that both, Summer and her aunt started laughing out loud.

Merlin noticed that Summer had the same tinkling laughter that May had. How very interesting, he thought.

Chapter 4

George and Iris Backer had a smooth trip across the channel, and the drive through to Holland had been reasonably straight forward. George would never get used to driving on the 'wrong' side of the road, though.

He and Iris were a bit concerned about leaving Summer with May. Although they knew she would be well looked after, they were more worried about the impression May would make on Summer with her herb potions. Yes, in their eyes, she was a bit eccentric - the way she dressed, for example, and her hair. Who wore their hair that length at May's age? Not one woman that George could recall. However, he still considered May to be a good-looking woman.

Still, he couldn't worry about that at the moment. His manager, Henney, had sounded quite desperate when he phoned. Very soon he would know first hand how much damage the vandals had done. When he pulled into the garden centre, Henney was there waiting for him.

"George and Iris, welcome. Did you have a good trip?" Henney asked in fluent English.

"Yes, yes, thanks," said George. "How bad is it, Henney?" he asked, getting straight to the point.

"As bad as it could possibly be," Henney replied. "The vandals just ran amok among the new experimental plants, hacking with knives at everything in sight. Then, with the rain, everything got soaked and it's all just lying in the muddy ground. Thank goodness most of our plants were in the greenhouses."

"I can't see our sponsors coming up with any more money at the moment for our experiments," George said

They had been trying various methods of grafting different plants and had achieved some success, but that was all ruined now.

"What do the local police say, Henney" asked Iris who had been standing very quiet during this exchange.

"They have no idea, I'm afraid. Several patrols have been keeping an eye out for us, but no luck so far," Henney replied despondently.

"Well there's nothing we can do at the moment, so we'll go on up to the house, if that's ok with you, Henney?" George said, starting the car again for the short drive.

"Yes, of course, make yourself at home. Lisa is there," Henney replied in his usual hale and hearty manner.

When the Backers came over to Holland, they always stayed with Henney and his wife. Henney met Lisa on a visit to England. They fell in love and had married within a few months.

Whilst unpacking the cases, Iris began to think about her sister May. They were different in so many ways, almost chalk and cheese at times. She sincerely hoped that May wasn't undoing all the good that she had done with Summer.

Chapter 5

Summer lay in bed thinking about what her aunt had said about Snoops, or 'Merlin' as she should call him now. He had ventured to the bottom of her bed and was curled up by her feet asleep. Having him on the bed was strangely comforting to her and, with that thought in her head, she drifted into sleep.

Well I don't have to do any more silly meowing, thought Merlin, *and I'm finally with my mistress Shasta*. With a deep sigh, he also drifted off to sleep.

In the next room, May lay quietly thinking about all that had happened during the day. It made her life easier knowing that Summer knew about Merlin. For a child of her age, she seemed to accept the strange news very well. Now the only problem was how to explain to Summer about Queen Abelia, and how they should meet. If necessary, she would do one of her spells. She would have to do one soon to turn Summer's hair blonde. Down in Faery Cove, everything red got burnt and she couldn't risk Summer going there with red hair. Oh well, that could wait until the morning. Then she too drifted into sleep.

On waking the following morning, May decided to brew herself some camomile tea. It always calmed her and cleared her mind. Whilst drinking her tea, May absentmindedly fingered her Chakra necklace, and then, calmly placing her right index finger over her third eye in the middle of her forehead, she waited for inspiration. It had never let her down before, but then this situation was so different. May finished her tea and took the cup over to the sink. The answer would come to her eventually.

"Good morning, Aunt".

"Goodness." She hadn't heard the child behind her and she was momentarily startled. It must be something to do with the gibbous moon. She disliked the time between the new and full moon, it was most disconcerting. Recovering herself, she said, "Good morning, my lovely. Did you sleep well?"

"Yes, thank you," said Summer brightly.

While Summer was eating her breakfast, May ventured to ask, "Do you like the colour of your hair, Summer?"

"Well, I don't really mind it. It's just that with red hair the sun burns my skin so much."

"How would you like blonde hair instead?"

Summer was surprised and excited by the question. It was what she had overheard Aunt May and Merlin discussing. "I would love it," she said.

"Well, when you have finished breakfast and the chores are done, we'll do it. That's settled," said May partly to herself.

Hurriedly, Summer finished her breakfast, put her cereal bowl by the sink to be washed and rushed into the bedroom to make her bed. Excited, she began to imagine herself with blonde hair. Caught up in her enthusiasm, Merlin jumped on the bed as she made it and rolled on his back for his tummy to be tickled.

"How do you think I will look with blonde hair, Merlin?" she asked.

"I'm sure it'll look lovely," said Merlin.

As the sun was so warm, May decided to change Summer's hair outside by the old well at the top of the garden. In readiness for the spell she had already combined equal quantities of white jasmine, white rose petals that had been kissed by the evening rain, and petals from the flower of equilibrium. To this she had added eight drops of rainwater and, on a whim, some oils. To her way of thinking, spells came mostly by instinct and experience. Shaking the potion together in a phial, she poured it onto Summer's hair whilst singing a rhyme quietly to herself, ending with 'so let it be'.

May was also aware that this magic hair tonic would clear Summer's mind and awaken her senses around her crown Chakra - the powerful energy point at the top of her head - preparing the way for telepathic insight. At the very least she would have great clarity, and perhaps even realise her true destiny. That would rely to a certain extent on Abelia, of course, and how much Summer was prepared to open her mind.

May wrapped Summer's hair in a towel to absorb the surplus water, gave it a quick rub and removed the towel. She gasped in amazement. Summer's hair had certainly grown during the time that she had been staying here but it now seemed much longer and the colour was beautiful.

"Oh, Summer, come and let's find you a mirror," she said. "I think you'll be very pleased."

They both hurried into the bedroom to look in the mirror. Summer was so surprised at the change in herself, she almost missed the chair and sat on the floor. Could that really be her, she wondered. She looked so different and so much older. Strangely, her hair had dried almost immediately and was now past her shoulders.

"What do you think?" asked her aunt.

"I...I... oh, Aunt May, I can't believe it. I look so different and I feel as if I should have always been blonde. It makes me look and feel so much older than I am."

"Oh yes, my Shasta., oh yes". May whispered silently.

Putting her arms round Summer, she pulled her up and they walked hand-in-hand into the sunlight of the garden. Merlin watched from a distance. 'Oh, my beloved, how enchanting you look,' he thought to himself. 'Shasta Day will be wonderful. I can feel it in my old bones.'

Chapter 6

May was aware that Summer would have to meet Abelia before long, but she wanted to prepare her first. Since she had changed Summer's hair to blonde, the child seemed not only to grow in height, but also to have matured into a beautiful young woman.

Summer seemed to have taken this in her stride, laughing many times when she had tried to fit into clothes and footwear that was much too small for her now. Consequently, May, with Summer's help, had done a few spells which provided Summer with new clothes and shoes. Sometimes they used conventional means; more often they just used magic. as the mood took them. Summer showed a natural aptitude for it all. May was aware of the strength of her magical powers but even she hadn't expected such a drastic change.

Oh yes, this was indeed Shasta reincarnated.

Thinking back, she had known this on the day Summer was born, even though she had red hair. She hadn't said anything to her sister, of course. May had looked into the baby's eyes and known, felt, that this was Shasta. She just couldn't wait for Shasta Day in the village. She, of course, would play a leading role, introducing Shasta to the villagers. In the past they had made do with a substitute; one of the local girls would take the part. This time they had the real thing.

The problem was should she now refer to Summer as Shasta or Summer? She would have to approach the child and seek out her feelings on the matter. No one in the village had remarked on the change in Summer. After all, this was Shasta, and magic was part of the history it was steeped in. However, only white magic was ever used, and only for the good of all mankind.

She decided to ask 'The Eye of Erasmus' as Summer was in bed, asleep. Merlin had been lying by Summer's feet but had now walked out to May.

"Come Merlin," May said, "let us light the candle and consult the book."

With that, Merlin followed May to her bedroom, his tail held aloft expectantly.

May faced her altar. As the sun had now fully set, she anointed her white candle with acacia oil and placed a bay leaf from her spice jar on the altar. Having already cut the appropriate flower from the garden in readiness, she placed it in a bowl of water beside the lit candle. Then she began to speak her usual incantation, finishing with "So let it be".

Burning the leaf in the candle's flame, May breathed in slowly and deeply six times. On the last breath out, she blew out the candle. Lifting up the book, she carried it across to her bed. The eye only became visible when the book was lifted up.

Erasmus lazily opened his eye.

"Good evening, May. I thought it was the child."

"Oh good evening, Erasmus, sorry to disturb you. You may go back to sleep. I'll do this myself this time but be assured the child will come."

Merlin lay beside her on the bed during this exchange of words. He was a bit wary of Erasmus.

"Well, Merlin, what shall we ask first"?

"Oh, I think we have to ask if we should call Summer Shasta, that is the most important thing," Merlin replied.

May phrased the question in her mind and the book flew open. They both looked at the rhyme and came up with the answer, "Yes, but don't force it."

"Well that certainly answers the question, May. Maybe we should talk to Summer in the morning."

"I think we had another question, Merlin, something to do with human form, I think.".

"Oh please, don't tease me, May, especially not now. I'd love to be human for Shasta Day, you know that. What are my chances, do you think? I would be happy with just one day as a human with my mistress, that's all I ask."

"Very well, are you ready?" asked May.

"Absolutely," said Merlin.

May concentrated on the question for him and again the book opened. This time the rhyme was easier but even she was startled by the answer.

"What does it say?" said Merlin.

"Oh I don't think you want to know, Merlin," said May.

"Please don't tease me, May. Tell me quick," Merlin almost shouted.

And May said, "The rhyme informs you to be prepared for the unexpected."

"Oh," said Merlin.

He didn't know what to make of that. Well he would just have to wait and see, but he didn't hold out much hope.

Chapter 7

"Well," said May the following morning after breakfast, the chores having been dealt with.,"I think it's about time we humoured your father and taught you something about plants, my dear. We could spend some time in the garden this morning. How would you like that?"

"I think that's a lovely idea, Aunt".

May noticed that even Summer's speech had matured but wisely decided not to remark on it. The difficulty was to remember not to call her Shasta yet. That would come soon enough, though. May walked ahead of Summer into the garden, towards the shed which stood to the side on its own. Ivy and honeysuckle had been encouraged to grow up over it so that it blended in with the rest of the garden. While May was in the shed picking up the gardening tools, Summer stood looking at the garden in awe. There were so many flowers and bushes of all descriptions. This encouraged her to wander around and she checked out each bush in case she missed something.

Unlike the garden at home, Aunt May's garden seemed to take on its own life, making its own decisions about what would grow and where. The path from the cottage meandered through the garden and invited you to walk down and admire everything to the left and right of it. Soft fruit bushes of peaches, blueberries and apricots grew in profusion everywhere. In some cases they were quite tall. This encouraged the likes of fuchsias and day lilies to peep around them, inviting the admirer to look beyond the bushes at them. Some sunflowers stood quietly erect, while others bent their heads to look at smaller plants below. Heavily perfumed jasmine and sweet peas climbed up anything that stood still long enough to support them. Here and there were mature trees of willow and oak which provided some relief from the relentless sunshine. Growing beneath the trees were primroses and forget-me-nots, intertwined with small bits of lavender which seemed to have sneaked in when no one was looking. Even Summer knew that it was very unusual for spring flowers to grow in the height of summer. In this garden there were no allowances made for the change in seasons. Everything grew as and when it felt the desire. Consequently there was a surprise at every twist and turn of the path.

Following quietly in her tracks were May and Merlin, reluctant to intrude on her solitude. Summer had so much to discover. Questions could be answered at a later time, if necessary.

To the left of her was a well with a small bucket and cup attached by a chain. Summer peered in at the water inside which was crystal clear. Feeling a need to quench her thirst, she dipped the cup in the well and filled it. As she bought it up to her mouth, she noticed that it seemed to shimmer in the sunlight. Curiously, she lifted the cup to her lips and drank thirstily. Although it was icy cold, she noticed that it had a kind of sweet taste. Refreshed, she looked to the end of the garden. Slightly off to the right she noticed a gate that she hadn't seen before. Wondering where it might lead, she walked towards it. Very gentle music seemed to emanate from the area, like tinkling bells ringing in the gentle breeze. May had many wind chimes in the garden but none of them sounded anything like this. She wouldn't have been at all surprised to see faeries and elves at work there.

"Get real, Summer, this is the real world". This was spoken by Summer out loud in a very mature womanly voice. "But this is Shasta, isn't it?" she said more softly to herself. Aunt May had said Faery Cove was around here somewhere at the bottom of the garden. As she put her hand on the gate, something stopped her from opening it. She began to feel hesitant and unsure of herself.

May, realising Summer's dilemma, said, "Have you enjoyed your wander round the garden? Merlin and I thought we would give you a chance to look around on your own for a while. What do you think?"

"I always thought my parents' garden was amazing, but this is so perfect, Aunt May, I feel as if I've always belonged here."

Inside, May felt a deep contentment, and Merlin beside her began to purr happily. The three of them turned in silence and began to wander back through the garden. Every so often, Summer would ask the name of a flower or May would point out various other plants, explaining what family they belonged to. At one point Summer passed a birdbath on the ground. It looked like an old up-turned dustbin lid filled with water. Inside were various large stones for birds to perch on to drink. It amused Summer to see frogs swimming in it, while others sunbathed on the stones. Some birds had taken the risk and were drinking beside them, while others formed an orderly queue, waiting their turn of pecking order. She was aware of a little robin which seemed to follow her movements with his head before feigning disinterest.

At one point May decided that a bit of weeding was called for. The two of them set about it in a companionable silence while Merlin lay beside them with his head resting on his paws, cat napping. Summer realised that, although the garden seemed exceptionally hot, she no longer seemed to burn as much since her hair had been changed to blonde. She was beginning to turn a deep tan and she embraced it.

"Does it ever rain here, Aunt May?"

"Yes, my child, but it's only very gentle rain, at night, just enough to give the flowers a drink. It can be very refreshing to walk in the rain. I frequently do it. Remember, Summer, the water of life is in a single raindrop. I think it's time we had a drink now. All this talk of water is making me feel thirsty."

"I think that would be lovely, thank you, Aunt," said Summer.

Together they walked up to the kitchen. Merlin, having woken and stretched, was following in their wake.

"I think we will have some lemonade," said May.

Going to the fridge to fetch the jug of lemonade, she realised that she hadn't made any.

"Oh dear, I seem to have forgotten to make any. How silly of me," she said. "Well, Summer, there seems to be only one solution, and that is to use a little bit of magic," said May. "Perhaps you would like to give it a try."

"I…. I…. well if you think I can, Aunt."

"I know you can," said her aunt. "It just takes confidence, that's all."

"What do I do first?"

"Cut the lemons in half," said May, "then squeeze the juice into the jug."

Summer did that and asked, "What next?"

"Add some sugar," said May. "You will know how much."

While she did this, May went to the herb garden outside the door and picked some mint.

"Now fill the jug with water, Summer, up to the brim." May meanwhile rinsed off the mint.

Summer automatically took the mint from her Aunt and dropped it into the jug. At the same time Summer whispered, "Lemonade be."

"What do I do now, Aunt?"

May laughed and said, "Well I don't know about you, Summer, but I am going to get a glass and drink some."

"But what about the little bit of magic?" Summer asked, feeling a bit deflated after all the effort.

"You've already done that," said May.

"But I haven't done anything," said Summer.

"Think back to when you dropped the mint into the jug. What did you say to yourself?"

"I don't remember saying anything at all," said Summer.

Of course the child wouldn't remember, thought May. *I have to forget that this is Shasta and think of her as Summer still.* This was a new experience for Summer but with her subconscious knowledge of her old ways, she would now automatically say the words. But the Summer of today wouldn't be aware of what she was doing yet.

Pouring out two glasses of lemonade, May sat pondering for a couple of moments. She had to remember that she was talking to a child, even though Summer's looks and manners belied that. She also seemed to be growing steadily on a daily basis.

May began to speak, choosing her words carefully. "When certain special people come to Shasta, my lovely, they automatically inherit the gift of the village which is to perform magic by spell casting. Mostly, they are not aware that this has happened to them. In some cases, chosen ones are also given the gift of second sight, which means that they can see what will happen in the future. This all happened to you when you came to stay here. The gift of second sight will mature over the time that you are here. Don't concern yourself too much, my love, it's all perfectly normal for Shasta. May I suggest that you have a bit of a lay down now with Primrose? Merlin is already in your room in the wicker chair, probably dreaming about a nice bit of fish."

This made Summer laugh and, with that, she made her way to her room. Merlin was indeed curled up in the wicker chair just as May had predicted. How did she know that? Maybe this was something to do with the second sight that May had been talking about. Slipping her feet out of her sandals, she pulled the patchwork cover over herself and lay down with Primrose.

She had many questions that she wanted to think about while she was laying here. Then maybe she would go to sleep. She certainly did feel tired. Yawning, she turned on her side and yielded herself to sleep. Unbeknown to her, Merlin had been awake, watching his beloved Shasta. *How beautiful she has grown*, he thought. Silently he jumped off of the wicker chair and padded across the room before jumping onto the foot of the bed. Curling up and settling himself, he gave a deep sigh and wondered if he would be human again for Shasta Night. With that thought he too drifted into sleep.

Later that evening, May was sitting in the garden on the swing seat, nibbling on a piece of cheese. The rain was just starting to fall gently and it was cooling to her skin after experiencing the heat of the sun all day. The night of the full moon always made her restless. Yes, it was expected that she should howl at it like the wolf, but she was getting to old for all that. She had lived too many lives. There had been at least five before this one. She would pay her respects to it later this evening. Somehow she felt that this would be the night for her beloved mistress to meet Abelia. She hadn't exactly told the truth about Merlin to Summer.

When the original Shasta had come to the village in her caravan all those years ago, May befriended her. Shasta and Merlin inevitably became quite fond of each other and .... *and that's enough of that thinking, May*, she told herself before paying her respects to the moon.

Chapter 8

Summer found it impossible to sleep that night; so many things were going through her head. She was dreaming that Merlin was human, a lovely thought but impossible. Lying on her stomach, she reached her arms out under the pillow and found something soft. Pulling it out, she discovered it was a little muslin bag filled with lavender.

I suppose it was put there by Aunt May to satisfy my energy needs and to give me wonderful dreams. That was the idea of lavender bags. Well how did I know that? thought Summer, and remembered the conversation she had had earlier with her aunt about the village giving privileges to certain people. She tried to go back to sleep but found it impossible. She was very hungry and had no idea what the time was. Come to think of it, she didn't recall having seen a clock here at all.

Quietly pulling back the covers, Summer got out of bed. Merlin remained undisturbed, although his tail was twitching back and forth which usually meant he was dreaming or anticipating something. Apart from that, he was snoring. Summer didn't realise that cats snored, and smiled to herself.

Tiptoeing out of the room, she made for the kitchen. As she passed her aunt's bedroom, she glanced in and saw that the bed was empty. It couldn't be that late, then, thought Summer to herself, otherwise her aunt would be in bed.

As she walked into the kitchen, her aunt walked in from outside. "Hello, my lovely, couldn't you sleep, then?"

"No," said Summer. "There seems to be something strange about tonight, but I don't know what it is and I feel very hungry," she said.

"Well," said her aunt, "it's a full moon tonight which makes it very special. In the olden days, we used to howl at the moon which was part of a ritual, but I'm getting too old for all that. Also I feel a bit silly howling at a moon these days. Now, you said you felt hungry. Is there anything special that you fancy?"

"Yes," said Summer, "lets go and look in the fridge to see what there is to be had."

"Let's not," said May. "This is Shasta remember. Just tell me what you fancy to eat and we'll see what we can conjure up."

"Well, to be honest, I fancy chicken, hot buttered bread and some sweet cakes to follow, all washed down with a glass of ginger beer," said Summer.

"Your word is my command, oh mistress" said May with a smile on her face.

Summer laughed and sat down at the kitchen table.

"Who is going to cook the chicken, Aunt?"

"No one, this is Shasta remember."

"Oh let me do this......"

Summer went to the range and looked at the oven door. She imagined a succulent juicy chicken in there. Within moments it appeared and smelt mouth-wateringly delicious. Picking up the oven gloves, she lifted the roasting tray out onto a trivet on the kitchen table. May watching her and laughed out loud. Summer joined in. The tinkling laughter of both women woke Merlin who stretched, yawned and jumped off the bed to see what all the fuss was about this late at night. He padded into the kitchen quietly and May, seeing him coming, explained what had happened.

"Well, as this seems a midnight feast, can I join in, then?" The women looked at one another to confirm their agreement.

"I don't see why not," they said in unison.

"We still need the hot bread and cakes," said Summer.

"My turn, then," said May. Staying at the table, she just glanced at the oven and there was suddenly a wonderful aroma of freshly baked bread and cakes.

Summer went to the oven with the oven gloves and took out the hot bread and newly baked sweet cakes. May, meanwhile, had gone to the fridge and produced a jug of ginger beer, which was ice cold, and the butter dish, which she put on the table.

"As this is a special occasion, Merlin, I will allow your dish to be on the table to enable you to eat with us, but don't think you can make a habit of this," said May.

"Thank you, May, I feel very honoured," he said, feeling that formality fitted the occasion.

Summer, being ravenously hungry, began to tear at the chicken. May firstly cut up some of the meat for Merlin, as he was incapable of helping himself as such, before joining her.

Having satisfied their hunger with all the food and drink, they sat back quietly for a while in an easy silence.

Summer eventually broke it by asking May about the Book of Erasmus. "Can I ask it some questions?"

"If you wish, my love," May answered. "Let's go to my room."

Summer was a bit hesitant as she followed May inside. Merlin had already made himself comfortable on the bed. May sat beside him, absentmindedly stroking him.

"Well, my child, pick up the book and bring it over to me."

Summer stared at the book. She wanted to pick it up but, at the same time, was frightened of doing so, not knowing why. Erasmus was asleep, but also aware of Summer's dilemma. He decided to wait a moment before speaking.

Summer ran her finger over the cover of the book.

"That tickles, Summer," said Erasmus, trying to put her at her ease, while having the reverse effect.

With a sharp intake of breath, she took her hand away, shaking slightly.

"Don't be worried," said May, "that's just old Erasmus and he won't hurt you. He's been the keeper of the book since time immemorial."

Summer picked up the book from the altar. With what seemed like practised ease, she held the book in her left hand, aware that

Erasmus was watching her. But she felt no fear this time. She thought about the questions that she wanted to ask but there were so many and wasn't sure which one to ask first. Her aunt had spoken about Faery Cove - perhaps that should be her first question.

She began to imagine faeries and what they would look like. Phrasing the question in her mind, she asked silently if there were faeries at the bottom of the garden. The book opened but she didn't understand the rhyme, so May helped her to decipher it.

The answer they came up with was, "Definitely."

The second question instantly sprung to mind. Getting used to asking the questions, she silently asked if she was Shasta. Amazingly she was sure she already knew the answer, but just needed confirmation. Her thoughts were confirmed in the answer.

The final question concerned Merlin. She was curious to know if he would become human again. This time she was nervous about looking at the answer. Supposing the book said no. She knew that he would be extremely disappointed and so would she. Why would that be, she wondered? Unable to stand the suspense any more, she awaited the answer which revealed itself as *Prepare for the unexpected.*

That can't be right, thought Summer, and asked the question again, only to receive the same answer. So what would be the unexpected, she thought. Closing the book still in deep thought, she was about to replace it on the altar when Erasmus asked, "What's the matter, my child. Your questions were answered, were they not?"

"Yes, Erasmus."

"Then why are you so confused? The book never lies."

"Yes, of course, you're right, Erasmus. Thank you," said Summer thoughtfully.

"Good night, Shasta."

"Good night, Erasmus."

May stopped stroking Merlin. Finally she knew that she could now refer to Summer as Shasta. Shasta (as she now truly believed she was) looked over to May and Merlin. As she walked towards her aunt, May stood up and opened her arms wide. Shasta ran towards her and was enfolded in May's love.

"Oh, my beautiful Shasta, my mistress, welcome back to your home," she said.

Merlin, watching this, purred noisily, his tail beginning to twitch back and forth. "Oh, but it was once me encircling her in my arms," he thought. "My darling Shasta, my heart longs for you so much I fear it will break. I will never ask anything again if I can but become human just one more time."

Chapter 9

May suggested that they went out to the garden as it was a beautiful night and everyone was now wide awake. Walking with Merlin by her side, Shasta began to realise how fond she was becoming of him. Bending down, she stopped to stroke him. Arching his back in delight, Merlin gave into the tender moment and wished for many more. May suggested that they should sit on the swing seat and view the garden by moonlight. Resting beside her aunt, Shasta began to think about all that had happened this evening. Cooking the food by magic, talking to Erasmus and having her questions answered - albeit not getting quite the answers she wanted - and lastly accepting that she was indeed Shasta.

While she sat pondering all these things, she was suddenly aware of a gentle rain falling about her. Although the flowers were drinking greedily, she and her aunt weren't getting wet at all, yet the rain was completely refreshing. Even Merlin's coat was still dry. In the light of the full moon, Summer could see right around the garden and down to the gate at the bottom. Even the bushes, which normally hid plants from view, seemed to be transparent.

Suddenly Shasta had an overwhelming desire to walk to the bottom of the garden.

"I think I will go for a walk, Aunt May. I have a lot to think about."

"Yes, of course, my lovely. When I have things on my mind, I always go down to Faery Cove. It seems to help me clear my mind."

As Shasta started to walk down the path, Merlin made to accompany her.

"Not this time, Merlin, this is one walk she must do alone. She is well protected and now is as good a time as any for her to meet Queen Abelia. We'll wait here for her return."

"Very good, May," he said but with some concern.

Shasta started to walk down the path, quietly moving in and

around the bushes. By now her aunt and Merlin were hidden from view. She didn't feel afraid as the full moon lit the whole garden. Looking around, she was aware that her aunt's garden was not overlooked at all, being completely surrounded by trees. Invisibly she walked among the flowers inhaling their heady perfume. Perhaps this had something to do with the gentle rain that was still falling.

Suddenly she heard what sounded like the tinkling of bells. At first she thought it was her aunt laughing but she was quite alone. Venturing further, she noticed in the distance a little circle of lights near the ground. Shasta was sure she could hear the sound of laughter. Moving faster, she headed for the lights which seemed to part into the shape of a semi-circle as she got closer.

What on earth can it be? she thought. Approaching with slight trepidation, Shasta stood just on the outside of the half-circle, watching.

"We have come to guide you to our Queen," a little voice said.

Looking down Shasta saw a little baby robin perched on a branch of a blueberry bush, his bright orange chest proudly thrust out.

"I'm sorry, what did you say?" Shasta asked, overcoming the surprise of talking to a bird.

"I said we have come to guide you to our Queen. Please put out the index finger of your left hand."

Dutifully Shasta did as she was asked and the robin flew onto her finger. With her right hand she gently caressed the bird's chest and wondered if it was the same robin she had seen previously at the birdbath. Reading her mind, the little robin told her that indeed he was the same and had been watching her for some time. It was his privilege, when the time was right, to guide her and the faeries to Queen Abelia.

He then flew towards her shoulder and perched there. Looking down, Shasta noticed that she now stood in a ring of lights. Although she was surrounded by moonlight, all around her was a kind of mystical orange glow.

Bending down with her hands on her knees, she looked towards the ground. From behind her a voice that she couldn't place told her to drink from the wishing well which stood a little way off. The robin flew off and perched on the cup expectantly. Shasta walked towards the well and, as the robin flew back to her shoulder, she once more drank the shimmering liquid. All of a sudden she began to feel quite strange. Her head began to buzz and she felt she needed to close her eyes to effect some relief. As she slowly opened her eyes again, she was aware of being back in the circle of light, but this time she could see all the little people quite clearly. What was even more amazing was that the flowers and bushes now seemed to tower over her.

My goodness, I'm reduced in height, she thought, as fear crept up her spine. So why hadn't that happened before when she had drunk it?

That wasn't important, though. She was now in the middle of the circle again and, looking around, she began to relax a bit. She could see the faeries quite clearly and it looked like there was a whole kingdom of them. Shasta was speechless. So it was true there were faeries at the bottom of the garden and that she could see them. One faery that was still quite a bit smaller than Shasta approached her timidly. Like the others, she was wearing a beautiful gossamer dress that looked like it had been spun by spiders. It was as yellow as a pale sun. Her hair was blonde and curly, and woven in and out of the curls was jasmine blossom and ivy. In her hand she held a small stem of jasmine.

"My name is Princess Jasmine," she said importantly.

"I'm very pleased to meet you," said Shasta.

Close behind Jasmine, waiting in line, was another. This one was wearing an identical dress to Jasmine but it was a bright orange. On top of her blonde hair was the bloom of a day lily. Much like Jasmine, this faery held a white flowering lily.

"My name is Princess Day Lily," she said equally importantly.

"I'm very pleased to meet you also," said Shasta.

One by one they came to introduce themselves. Shasta noted that all the faeries were similarly dressed. Interwoven in their hair were various flowers depending on which flower they represented. She had never seen such a wondrous sight. Apart from the two princesses, each of the faeries carried paper lanterns lit by glow-worms. As each faery moved, a faint dust of all the colours of the rainbow seemed to fall about them.

"Now all the introductions have been made, it's my turn," said a voice to the right of Shasta. Although she had been reduced in size, she still found she had to bend down to hear the faeries. She bent once again to listen to this new arrival.

"Hello," said Shasta, "and what is your name?"

"My name is Evening Primrose, and I'm first in command after Queen Abelia."

She was dressed in a brighter yellow dress than Princess Jasmine and the bloom of an evening primrose perched jauntily on the side of her head. It seemed to be just balanced there. She was also carrying a stem of the evening primrose which seemed to glow so much brighter in the moonlight.

As she swiftly turned round, a cloud of faery dust emitted from her dress. It was a bit like rainbow coloured pollen being scattered in the air.

"Come," she said, "we must not keep the Queen waiting."

Surrounding Shasta the faeries began singing and dancing as they glided along, their beautiful voices like wind chimes tinkling in the breeze, whilst the glow from the paper lanterns lit the way in the darkness.

Finally they reached the gate at the bottom of the garden. It swung open as they neared it. Once they were all through, it silently closed again. Still perched on Shasta's shoulder was the little robin singing sweetly in her ear.

So many things had happened to Shasta recently, she was almost tempted to ask if one of them was the tooth faery, but thought better of it. This didn't seem to be the time. Finally everyone stopped at the base of a tree. Growing around it was lavender and forget-me-nots along with blue and white bells. Hedra Ivy meandered in and out, where permitted. Looking closely on the ground, Shasta noticed many toadstools around the base of the tree. Other faeries seemed to occupy these. If she crouched down low enough, she could see inside. They seemed to be set out like normal houses with little tables, chairs and beds.

"What else did you expect?" said a voice.

Shasta felt as if her mind had been read.

"I didn't mean to be rude," said Shasta standing up.

"Stay where you are on the ground. Don't you know you are in the presence of the Queen Abelia?" said Evening Primrose with as much importance as she could summon.

Shasta knelt where she was. A few yards in front of her was the prettiest faery of all. She was quite a bit smaller than Shasta.

Queen Abelia was wearing a silver dress which shimmered in the moonlight, Shasta's first impression being that spiders had spun it onto her body as she stood.

Unlike the other faeries, her dress reached to the ground. Her feet were encased in silver and gold slippers, and she held a wand which seemed to be similar in colour and style to silver Christmas tinsel. To complete her regalia, Abelia wore a crown of silver and gold, encrusted with tiny hanging crystals.

Behind the Queen was a throne made from a lavender bush which she now sat on. The two princesses, Jasmine and Day Lily, sat on the ground on either side while Evening Primrose stood behind with a fern in her hand, gently waving it up and down in homage.

There was a sudden hush as the Queen spoke.

"Welcome to my kingdom, Shasta. I have waited many, many years for your return."

Shasta began to question herself. Not only was she in a faery kingdom, the Queen of all the faeries was talking to her as if she had always known her. What did she mean by many, many years, she wondered.

"I realise that you must find this all very difficult to take in. It's not every night that you get to visit a faery kingdom and meet a queen," said Abelia, "but you can't begin to imagine how happy I am to have you here at last."

"I just don't understand, your majesty," said Shasta

"Oh, please call me Abelia. I don't like too much ceremony here, although some of the faeries do take their duties rather seriously at times."

A delicate cough came from Evening Primrose standing behind them.

"Let me try and explain, then, my dear," said Abelia. "I know May told you the legend of Shasta when you visited the village recently."

"Yes," said Shasta. "I'd forgotten you knew my aunt."

"Oh, my dear, May is a regular visitor here. She comes here to think, usually long after everyone else is in bed asleep."

"I had no idea," said Shasta almost to herself.

Carrying on as if there had been no interruption, Abelia said, "The Shasta in the village legend is you. Let me try and explain. In the past, when the village was originally named after you, May, as she was also known then, asked you to go and live with her and Merlin. Over time you fell in love with Merlin but for reasons I won't go into now, neither of you had a chance to live your lives together. Fate has intervened on this rare occasion and allowed you a second chance in this life. May was also given the opportunity to relive another life as she is an integral part of the story. When Merlin appeared on her doorstep, he told her the sad story of how he had been turned into a cat. Taking pity, she took him in to live with her and he's lived there to this day."

While Shasta was coming to terms with all that Abelia had told her, Abelia called Princess Jasmine to her side.

"Get her a drink from the well, please, Jasmine."

"Yes, your majesty," Jasmine said.

Because the cup was attached to the well, Jasmine had used an acorn cup to collect the water and she invited Shasta to drink. Although the acorn cup was only tiny, it seemed to replenish itself with enough water to quench Shasta's thirst.

"It will soon be dawn," said Abelia. "You have to get back to May and Merlin. Please remember this one last thing, Shasta. You'll be the Queen on Shasta day and the faeries always dress the Shasta Queen, so I'll see you again then. Don't forget"

"I won't," she said.

Surely I haven't been here all night, thought Shasta, but the sky was beginning to get light, so she must have been. Saying goodbye to Abelia and all the other faeries, she began to make her way back through the gate.

"If you ever need any advice, Shasta, come and see me. This is your village and heritage."

"Thank you, Abelia. I'll remember that."

Whilst she was walking back through the gate, the robin returned and settled on her shoulder.

"All is well then, Shasta?" the robin asked.

"I really don't know," she said. "There is so much I have to think about." *My beloved Merlin*, she thought aloud. *Now I understand why I feel so close to him. Some things are starting to make sense.*

Walking back up the path wearily, she came to the swing seat. Still sitting there was her faithfully Merlin.

"Oh, Merlin," she said.

"Ah, you have spoken to Abelia, then?"

"Yes," she said softly. "I had no idea about us in the past."

"How could you, my dearest mistress? But what is meant to be will be," he said.

With that, she walked into the kitchen and made her way to her bedroom, tiptoing quietly past her aunts' room and into her own. Climbing into bed she began to think about all that Abelia had said to her. Merlin had followed her in and, as usual, had curled up at the foot of the bed.

With that, Shasta fell into a troubled sleep. Her last thought before sleep overtook her was what Merlin would look like in human form.

Merlin's' last thought before sleep was what did the Book of Erasmus mean by 'prepare for the unexpected'? Even Erasmus couldn't give an answer to that.

May was lying awake in her room. She had only been feigning sleep as Shasta crept past. By now Abelia would have told her about the love between her and Merlin. Maybe she was only eight and three quarters living outside the village, but here in Shasta she had aged to at least eighteen years old. Maybe the Book of Erasmus would come up with the right answer. *Only time will tell*, she thought. With that in mind she drifted into sleep.

Chapter 10

Both May and Shasta woke late the next morning. Having discussed all that had happened in Faery Cove, they had finally got round to having their breakfast and completing the usual chores of washing up the dishes and making the beds. Housework was rarely done in Shasta Village except by the swish of the magic finger or just a thought process.

"Shall we take a walk in the village and look at the preparations for Shasta Day? It'll soon be upon us," suggested May

"Yes, please," said Shasta. "I'd like that very much."

Walking down to the village, they sat in the shade drinking orange juice and watching the preparations getting under way. Shasta began to get very excited. She was aware that she was getting second glances and, in some cases stares, but it didn't bother her. May hadn't commented, so why should she worry? The village had heard the rumour that the Shasta from the old legend had returned, and this niece of May's held a striking resemblance to the way Shasta had generally been depicted, but the villagers were afraid to approach and ask in case they looked foolish.

No explanation was offered by May and she was enjoying herself.

No one knew of course that May had planted a thought in the shopkeepers' minds, suggesting that the original Shasta might return this time.

The buzz of excitement and gossip outside the shop had started to become exaggerated and the story at the moment was that Shasta was returning to her village. Because there was a faint chance that May's niece could be Shasta, the villagers had decided to celebrate in the old original way.

The whole community had chosen a tree, and past custom dictated that it should be cut down and brought through the village in solemn procession. This would happen the day before the celebration. It would be erected in the middle of the green and would be stripped of its branches and leaves. At the top of the tree was placed a crown from which hung multi-coloured ribbons. Each Morris dancer would take hold of a ribbon and, by dancing in an intricate pattern, the ribbons would be woven around the tree until they reached the bottom.

Although August was in the summer period, the moon also governed the celebration. Litha time, or Weodmonath – weed month - was held to celebrate the village changing from a weed infested place to a haven of beautiful gardens and hedgerows. This was thanks to the goodness of Shasta. So to have Shasta returning was ensure an even more joyous occasion.

May and Shasta had talked about what they would cook, but no final decision had been made yet. It wasn't surprising that food was so easily prepared for this festival. If one only had to wish it to be cooked and it was, there surely couldn't be any problem. It was apparently quite normal to roast a ram or bull so that everyone would be fed. These, of course, had to be caught first. It could be done by magic but that would take the fun out of the chase. Occasionally a suckling pig from the village was roasted, but bulls and rams were the preferred dish.

Having finished their drinks, May and Shasta began to make their way back to the cottage. Waiting at the gate for them was the ever-faithful Merlin. Giving him a stroke, Shasta and May walked under the rose arch into the garden and through to the kitchen. There was so much to do; finalising their plans for the food for instance. Ok, so they only had to think of something and it would be cooked by magic, but part of the excitement was making the decisions. Also, another important factor to consider was how she and May would be dressed. May had made her decision on what she would wear, but they would have to go to Faery Cove to collect Shasta's dress which was to be made by the faeries.

Normally faeries only appear at night, but Abelia had given

permission on this occasion for them to be about during the morning. Providing that May and Shasta went to Faery Cove just before dawn they would stay visible.

Chapter 11

Shasta woke up early the following morning, the eve of Shasta Day. In a past life she had instigated all of this and these were her people. Shasta Day meant so much to them. How strange it all felt but it was a fact.

Thinking back, it was only two weeks ago that she had arrived in Shasta as Summer Backer, a young schoolgirl in the spring of her life, arranging sleepovers with friends, spending half the night giggling over schoolboy heroes and comparing them to unobtainable pop stars.

Now she knew not only was she Summer Backer in this life but previously she had been Shasta, a legendary folk heroine of this village who had been in love with a young man called Merlin. He was now alive in this life (and maybe others) as a cat, and living with her Aunt May. In this magical world, she could visit a faery kingdom overseen by Queen Abelia, and to reach there she just had to diminish in size and be guided by a robin and a stream of faeries who were the prettiest folk she had ever seen. On top of all that, she had something called 'second sight' which enabled her to see into the future. This had still to be proven, though. The gift that disturbed her most was the thought that whatever she decided ought to happen in Shasta would take place. That in itself was a tremendous responsibility.

She suddenly felt very guilty. Not once had she thought about her parents. However they had said that they would write to her or phone and they hadn't. So perhaps they had been too preoccupied with the problems at the garden centre and with catching up with Henney and Lisa.

From the kitchen came the lovely aroma of coffee and toast, which meant that May was already up and about. Maybe she would have coffee and toast this morning. Cereal and juice didn't seem to appeal to her much these days.

Shasta was aware that Merlin was lying at the bottom of the bed and tentatively moved her foot to see what would happen. As she did so, Merlin moved with her so that he could maintain contact. "My beloved Merlin," she thought.

Well she couldn't lie here all day. There was so much to do. Throwing the bed covers back, much to Merlin's disgust, she slipped her feet into her slippers and pulled on her dressing gown. Merlin jumped down and started to wash himself with his paw. This always amused Shasta, and she laughed. Her aunt was sitting at the table sipping her coffee as she walked into the kitchen.

"Good morning, Aunt, what a wonderful day," she said.

"Good morning, my lovely, and yes I agree with you, it certainly is," May replied. "Would you like your usual cereal and juice Shasta?"

"No, thank you, Aunt. I thought I would join you in coffee and toast this morning."

No sooner was the remark out of her mouth than the coffee and toast appeared in front of her. Shasta accepted this as part of normal life now to the extent that she asked her aunt if she would like to join her in another cup of coffee.

"Yes, please," said May and it appeared.

They both laughed conspiratorially.

Merlin, joining them, asked if he could have coffee and toast too.

"Don't be silly, Merlin, you're a cat," said Shasta and instantly regretted it as he appeared to flinch.

"I have some nice juicy fish for you this morning, Merlin. How does that sound?"

"Oh I suppose it will have to do, May. After all, I'm only a cat!"

With that he flounced outside into the garden and sat under the bushes.

"I think I've upset him, May," said Shasta. "I didn't mean to."

"Oh, I shouldn't worry too much about that," said May and

instantly produced the fish. Merlin, on smelling it, was slowly tempted back again. Making a very half-hearted attempt, he only ate a bit of it and walked off again. May realising instantly what the problem was decided not to discuss it with Shasta. No point in upsetting her even more. Merlin was obviously still in love with Shasta but, as a cat, he could only think about it. May felt very sad but there was nothing that she could do for him. Shasta's power was much stronger than hers now, even though she didn't realise it yet. Only she could change the way things were and it had to be her decision not May's. In her heart she would love to see Merlin in human form again. He was a very handsome young man and, in a past life, she had probably been a little bit in love with him herself. Her desire now would be to see Shasta and Merlin together in love, and she would be mistress to both of them.

If only it was in my power, thought May.

"If only what was in your power, Aunt May?" asked Shasta.

Not realising that she had made the comment out loud, May brushed it aside by saying, "Oh it's just me being silly, my dear. Don't mind me. Well," said May more composed now, "shall we clear up the dishes, do the other chores and go down to the village? It's the tree ceremony today."

"Oh yes," said Shasta feeling youthful excitement. "You can explain it to me on the way, Aunt".

They both took a slow walk down to the village. Although it was still quite early, there were many villagers about, bustling here and there with an air of excitement. Every so often, one of the men would touch their forelock to Shasta in a respectful way. At times she was torn between amusement and curiosity. As before, May secretly smiled to herself but made no comment.

Standing at the edge of the village green, they became aware of cheering. In the tradition of the legend, the villagers came into sight carrying a tree that had been felled. It was being carried by at least ten men, with others following in its wake. The children having now returned from their boarding schools, danced around the men, sometimes getting in the way and pulling at the branches. Everyone was eager to be involved. The women formed two rows facing each other at the edge of the green. May and Shasta tagged on at the end, not wanting to be left out. As the men reached the two rows of women, there was a sudden hush. Each woman touched a part of the tree as it was lifted past, including May. Shasta not really knowing why, touched it anyway. Its leaves felt cool to the touch and she felt the urge to bury her face in them. They smelt of pine and earth. She gave into the impulse and there was an audible gasp from the villagers.

"It be true," said one.

"It's Shasta herself come back," said another.

One by one they began mumbling in awe among themselves. Shasta, raising her head, began to feel a bit embarrassed at what she had done, but it felt right and it smelt so beautiful. Then she became aware that everyone was staring at her.

She looked at May for reassurance.

"Go with your heritage, my dear," was all Aunt May said. Only the real Shasta would have dared do that this, being a sacred tree and all," said one man.

"No one would dare after the ritual has been done in the forest," said another.

Shasta walked slightly away from the crowd and turned her back on them. What she had done had felt natural. Had she done it before? Mental images of the past began to swim in her mind. She herself had ordered a tree to be cut down, she now knew. The sacred ritual for purification of the earth by a female entering puberty was then performed. On completion of the ritual, she, Shasta, had buried her head in the leaves in utter delight at being at one with nature. This was her privilege alone. The tree was then carried through the village and erected on the green in celebration....

The crowd stood expectantly awaiting her.

Turning, she raised her arms for silence and said to them, "People of Shasta, I AM the Shasta you speak of. Do not be afraid, I have returned to my village to celebrate with you. This Shasta Day will be one to remember ever after. We will feast and drink for two days instead of one. There will be sporting games and music, and ale will flow freely. All the houses will be decked out with flowers and greenery. I give permission for branches of trees to be cut and planted over doors according to the old traditions. The maidens will wear their finest colourful dresses and garlands of flowers and ribbons in their hair. The young men will all present their loved ones with ribbons as a token of their love. So it is decreed. Now let us begin the celebrations by erecting the tree."

With rapturous cheering ringing in her ears, Shasta looked across to May who seemed different somehow. As she got nearer she could see tears in May's eyes but with a serene countenance to her face.

"Did I get it right, Aunt May? It felt right to me".

"Oh, my Shasta, my mistress," said May, bending down and kissing the hem of Shasta's dress.

Shasta pulled her to her feet.

"Never go on your knees to me, Aunt May. I'm not worthy of it".

With that she slipped her arm through her aunt's and watched the tree being stripped of its branches and secured in place. As the men began to raise the tree, they sang the ancient words of old.

Once the tree had been secured in place, two strong young men came forward. One made ready to take the weight of the other who climbed on his shoulders and fixed the crown to the top. The women had already attached the ribbons, which were now hanging down from the crown. As Shasta watched this, slowly past memories returned in full. Nothing more would be done now until the next day when the Morris dancers would begin the dance to start the fair. Shasta hoped that Merlin would have returned by the time that they got back. It was now well into the afternoon and they had been gone since early morning.

She and May walked back to the cottage but there was no sign of Merlin waiting by the gate as usual. *Strange*, thought May, *he doesn't usually sulk this long. Maybe he's in the garden.*

Shasta was also concerned. She really hadn't meant to upset him this morning with that silly remark about him being a cat. If he couldn't be found in the garden, then she would be really concerned. May tried to tempt him with the smell of his favourite food, but there was no sign of him.

"I expect he will turn up when he is ready," said May. "Don't worry too much, Shasta."

Later that evening, as she sat in the swing seat with May, she felt as if half of her was missing. She missed Merlin so much. If he returned to his human form, she knew that she would fall in love with him all over again. May sat quietly, thinking about the day but also knowing what was going though Shasta's mind.

She had been so proud of her niece taking command as she had. The reverence of the villagers hadn't surprised her one bit. Shasta, being a magic village, also meant that they revered the legends of old, and to have Shasta in their midst was a hope come true for them. They would tell the story to their grandchildren, she was sure.

The next two days would indeed be joyous, if only Merlin would return. The only time he had disappeared before was when May had upset him and he had returned the following day, feeling very apologetic. They had both agreed that they would not let it happen again. Merlin was feeling very vulnerable at the moment, now that Shasta had returned. May knew that he was finding it very difficult to come to terms with being a cat and yet still in love with Shasta. Hopefully the Book of Erasmus would rectify that. It had said *prepare for the unexpected.* Tonight May would leave the cottage door open in case he returned late at night.

Their contribution of food for the fair had already been dealt with. They had decided on several chickens, hot bread and revel cakes. The cakes they had made in the conventional way when they had returned from the village. In fun they had blown the flour at each other. Both had ended up with white faces by the time the cakes were ready for the oven. Dark flour was blended with currants and caraway seeds. Afterwards they were cooked and left to cool. Each cake was then sliced and four pieces from each were kept for good luck. One of the pieces Shasta put to one side for herself, hoping that the good luck in this case would be Merlin returning. Tomorrow morning first thing, they would have to be in Faery Cove to try on the dress the faeries were making for her.

"May I suggest we retire to bed, mistress? We have to be in Faery Cove early in the morning and Merlin will be quite safe, I'm sure. Don't worry too much."

Shasta accepted the old ways very quickly, but she looked on May as an equal not a servant, and said so.

"Thank you, mistress," said May, "but I'm very happy this way."

"Very well," said Shasta, "but you are still my Aunt May."

With that, Shasta retired to bed.

Climbing into bed, she missed the comfort of Merlin at her feet. She hadn't meant to upset him. How could she have been so stupid? Shasta spent a very restless night tossing and turning, imagining all the terrible things that could be happening to Merlin.

Chapter 12

While Shasta and May had been in the village, Merlin had been keeping close watch on them from a distance. He was very hurt by the remark of Shasta. Before Summer, as she was, came to stay, he had already accepted his role in this life too as a cat and had been content with that. After all, he was living with May. Should he really ask for more?

Now, with Shasta back, it had disturbed all his thoughts and he desperately wanted to be human again. He had been a cat in her life for quite long enough. The thought of putting his arms around her and holding her again was driving him mad. No one could possibly understand his feelings. The closest he came was to lie by her feet on the bed.

He had taken himself out to the forest to think and witnessed the cutting down of the tree. Wandering down to the village, but keeping under cover, he had seen the speech made by his beloved Shasta to her people. How could he stand a chance if he was still a cat? He felt sure that Shasta had feelings for him but was it as a cat or a human? Feeling hungry, he was tempted back to May's cottage. She would have left him something to eat. So slowly, but with a heavy heart, he made his way back. On reaching the back garden he could see the door was still open. May was sitting in the swing seat, and obviously Shasta had gone to bed.

"Hello, May," he said.

"Merlin, I was getting a bit concerned about you. Come and sit beside me." Merlin jumped up beside May.

"Oh, May, what a day I've had. I know it was silly of me to get upset but I can't stop remembering when I was once human and Shasta and I were lovers. I still love her so and I find this so hard to cope with. To be punished in our previous lives together was bad enough, but to be punished again and for eternity ...."

Merlin was so upset May stroked his fur as compensation. She knew it wouldn't help but it might make him feel loved.

"You must be hungry, Merlin. I have prepared your favourite food," said May. "Come and try to eat something."

"I am hungry, May. I haven't eaten all day. Thank you for going to the trouble," he said.

Having eaten the food May had prepared, Merlin made his way to Shasta's bedroom. She seemed to be thrashing about in the bed in the throws of a nightmare. Jumping onto the bed, he settled by her feet. Almost at once she seemed to calm down. Well if this was the way it was meant to be, at least he was beside his beloved mistress. With this thought in mind, he settled into a fitful sleep.

Merlin woke again. Why was he so restless? He jumped silently off the bed and went to the back door. It was open, which meant May was still sitting outside.

"Goodness you made me jump, Merlin. I didn't feel your presence," said May.

"Sorry, May, I just feel really strange and thought I would go for a walk to the bottom of the garden," he said.

"Very well, Merlin. Would you like some company?" she asked.

"Perhaps just to the gate, May, that would be nice."

As they walked through the garden in the gentle rain, they maintained a thoughtful silence. May wished she had the power to change the situation but that would mean changing the past. Merlin was wishing against all the odds that he could become human again. As they reached the bottom gate by the well, May left him and returned to the cottage. Merlin felt very lonely as May walked away. In many ways she was his main link to the past, even though his love was for Shasta. Realising he was by the well, he decided to visit Faery Cove so, jumping up, he lapped some water, taking care not to fall in. He still had to become smaller to visit the faeries. His normal size would frighten them, even though they were used to him. Feeling himself changing, he walked towards the gate and was welcomed by the circle of light. As he got nearer, the lights seemed to retreat from him. Strange, he thought to himself, they have never been frightened by me before.

"Halt, who goes there?" said Evening Primrose.

"It's me, Merlin. Why are you challenging me?" he said.

"Merlin is a cat and why are you walking around on all fours?" she said.

"Because I AM a cat," said Merlin. "That's what we do."

"Since when were cats given human form and why are you unclothed? Now will you please tell me why you're in Faery Cove?" challenged Evening Primrose agitatedly.

The truth suddenly dawned on Merlin. Could it be? Was it possible? He was frightened and closed his eyes. When he could stand the suspense no longer, he opened them. First he looked at his front paws. They were dirty but they looked like hands. Then he turned to look behind him and, yes, his back paws seemed to be feet. Jumping up, he began to run about wildly, laughing fit to burst.

"Are you going to continue in this unseemly behaviour, especially unclothed?" asked Evening Primrose.

Realising his predicament, Merlin was somewhat overcome and tried to cover up. "Evening Primrose, I can assure you it really is me, Merlin. I asked the Book of Erasmus if I would become human again and it said 'prepare for the unexpected.' I suppose this is the unexpected."

Still a bit unsure of things, Evening Primrose allowed him into the circle. As first in command after the Queen, she had to show some sort of authority.

"Very well," she said, "who is the Faery Queen?"

"Abelia, of course," he answered without hesitation.

"Well, it seems you may be Merlin in human form after all, then." She said. "Follow us back to the kingdom, but first of all at least try and cover yourself with a fern of some sort, please. Your form is most distressing to the eye."

Merlin, hearing the titters of laughter around him, pulled at the nearest fern which seemed to just cover his embarrassment. The feeling of being human again and walking upright was beyond imagination. He was so happy he wanted to cry, but first he had to see Abelia and talk with her.

They walked in procession down to the kingdom, the faeries seemingly amused by his predicament. Queen Abelia, who was aware of everything that happened in the kingdom, was sitting pondering. "So, history repeats itself and Merlin is human again," she said quietly to herself.

With these thoughts on her mind, she was aware of a bit of a commotion outside her palace. *Ah, they have arrived*, she thought. Evening Primrose was about to advise her of the fact but, anticipating this, she rose and walked outside.

"Good evening, Merlin," she said.

"Good evening, Abelia. Please excuse my informal dress," he replied, trying to ensure that the fern covered most of him. "I was taken a bit by surprise, as you can see."

With an amused grin, she agreed and beckoned him into her toadstool.

Seated inside, they were comfortable in each other's company. Merlin had visited many times but usually in his form as a cat.

"I cannot believe how fortunate I am, Abelia," said Merlin. "I really never expected this to happen again and I can't express my relief. This means that I will be able to join in with Shasta and May tomorrow, but as a human."

"I'm really pleased for you, Merlin. I know how much you wanted this moment to happen. Your fate is still in Shasta's hands, though, as you know," Abelia replied softly. "If you are going to attend the fair tomorrow, then I think we have to make you some clothes. I think surprise is the element here, Merlin. Maybe you could stay here until after Shasta and May have been. They will be coming just before dawn."

"Thank you, Abelia, I do feel slightly silly with only a fern to protect my embarrassment."

Abelia laughed with him. It was so lovely to see him happy again and with a purpose. She wondered at the same time what Shasta would make of the situation. After all Merlin was a very handsome lad and they were very much of the same age. He looked exactly as he did in his previous life before he was transformed into a cat, but then why wouldn't he?

Rising to her feet, Abelia walked outside. "Faeries, I have an announcement to make," she said.

At once there was a complete silence.

"We have an unexpected surprise in the kingdom. As many of you know, Merlin was originally human. He became a cat, and now, because of Shasta returning to the village, he has taken on human form again. We need to ensure that he is correctly dressed when he meets Shasta at the fair today."

With this last remark there was a general titter among the faeries who found the situation rather unusual. For a human he was an exceptionally handsome lad. His blonde hair was quite long, and curled under at the edges. They had to ensure that he was dressed to enhance his best features, and all this before Shasta and May arrived before dawn. It would be a long night.

Merlin was ecstatic. He couldn't believe that The Eye of Erasmus had granted him this one wish. He didn't stop to consider why, only that however long it lasted he would be happy. To be able to hold Shasta in his arms again would be wonderful. He just hoped that she would feel the same.

The faeries decided to dress him in traditional costume in a short dark blue velvet doublet with the front open to the waist. This was laced across with satin ribbon. Underneath this he wore a white shirt which was embroidered at the neck. The sleeves of the doublet were slashed between the elbows and wrist, and tied in three places with silk. There were long tights and a soft dark blue velvet cap decorated with a large feather. The finishing touches were a short matching velvet cloak and soft pointed black shoes.

Abelia came to look at the transformation in Merlin. He was indeed a handsome youth but for now he had to be hidden away, at least until Shasta and May had been and gone. She didn't want to lose the element of surprise.

"Faeries, until Shasta and May have left the kingdom, Merlin is our secret, is that understood?" she announced to all assembled.

"Yes, your majesty," they said in unison.

"Merlin, I think it would be better if you stayed in the guest toadstool for the time being until after Shasta has gone."

"Very well, Abelia" he said, finding it very hard to curb his enthusiasm.

It would be a very long wait.

Chapter 13

It was still very dark when May woke the next morning. Rising, she looked at the moon which was still shining. She preferred the nightly comfort of the moon and the stars through open curtains. The gentle rain heard through the slightly open window lulled her to sleep at night. There would be no need to wake Shasta yet. May had heard her through the night restlessly tossing back and forth. Her body was calm when Merlin had lain by her feet. Then the endless thrashing again when he had left her.

May knew that Shasta had the power to make things right with her and Merlin by simply wishing it, but this had to be something she discovered in her own time. It wasn't May's place to advise her now. She had reverted to the mistress again, regardless of how kindly Shasta looked upon her. Shasta's magical powers would have far superseded hers by now and this would become self-evident over the next few days. May's renewed role was to be her gentle adviser. If pushed by Shasta she would always be there to comfort her, if she needed it.

What a beautiful girl she had become, thought May in reflection, both in looks and in her gentle nature. May felt she had gone back in time.

"Oh, if only we could go back in reality, all would be so much easier," she mused.

She went out through the kitchen to the swing seat and sat down with a cup of coffee. This would always be her favourite place, she thought, where she had a beautiful view of the whole garden. Even in the moonlight the flowers were shown off to their best advantage. They seemed to take on a different look somehow. Knowing that Merlin was now safe, she could relax. She knew he would go to visit Abelia and talk things over with her. Strange that he hadn't come back again, though.

"Oh well," thought May, "I had better wake Shasta if we're to be at Faery Cove in time." As she stood up, Shasta was standing beside her.

"My goodness, child, you scared me," said May.

"I'm so sorry, Aunt, I didn't mean to. I was having trouble sleeping and we have to be at Faery Cove before dawn. Will you sit down beside me and talk while I have a cup of coffee?" she asked whilst automatically putting her hand out to receive the cup.

Sitting back down, May allowed Shasta to rest her head against her shoulder. As she did this Shasta burst into tears.

"Oh, May, I miss Merlin so much. Oh that he had his wish to become human again. I would be so happy for him."

"Hush, child, all things will come to pass, trust me in this."

"Let's go and talk to Abelia and get you dressed for your day. Remember you declared two days of celebration."

"So I did," said Shasta, suddenly brighter. Once her coffee was finished, they both headed back inside.

Dressing themselves, they made their way to the bottom of the garden to the well. As they drank the water they felt the familiar feeling come over them as they shrunk in size. Going through the gate they met Evening Primrose on the other side.

"May and Shasta! I was beginning to think you wouldn't come. Hurry, there is no time to lose. So many things have happened. Oh, it's so wonderful and I'm under orders not to tell you, so I can't. Hurry up," she added excitedly.

Shasta, although feeling sad inside, was amused and, in spite of this, laughed out loud. May was more thoughtful. What had happened, she wondered, to get Evening Primrose so flustered and excited? Could her wildest dreams have come true? She felt a warm glow inside and was convinced that this was so. Through her power of second sight, May suddenly had a vision of Merlin in one of the guest toadstools, hiding. He was human again and dressed in finery.

So the Eye of Erasmus had been right once again.

She had to put her fist to her mouth to stop shouting out in glee. She couldn't let Shasta know what she had seen. If he was hiding in the guest toadstool, then Abelia had intended it as a surprise and she wasn't going to spoil that.

With a light heart she followed Shasta and Evening Primrose to the faery kingdom and Abelia's presence.

She began quietly to hum a tune to herself as they walked along.

"You seem happy, May," said Shasta.

"Oh I have a good feeling about this fair, Shasta. I believe all will come out right in the end."

"I do hope so," said Shasta. "You are so wise, May. I want you to be right".

Abelia, aware that they were coming, had already warned Merlin to stay hidden inside the toadstool. Besides, Shasta's dress was to be a surprise.

"Very well," said Merlin. "I'm looking forward to dancing with her. After all, it has been at least two hundred years since I last held her in my arms."

Evening Primrose arrived with May and Shasta, and presented them to Abelia.

"My friends," Abelia said, "we have much to do before dawn, so let us get started. Faeries, let us begin to dress our beautiful Shasta for the fair."

On this instruction, they started work on the dress.

The inspiration for the dress had come from the shaft of light given off by the moonlight. It was to be full length, cut deep at the back and front, with full sleeves that finished at the fingertips. The faeries, assisted by millions of silk worms and spiders, would help spin it, ensuring that it would be gossamer thin and kissed by the early morning dew as the sun rose in the sky. The colour would be sky blue to match Shasta's eyes, and threaded with pure silver and diamonds. On Shasta's feet would be slippers of blue and silver with a small thin heel. They would sparkle in the moonlight because the faeries would cover them in rainbow faery dust. Woven in her hair would be tiny blue forget-me-nots and small white Shasta daisies. Then the long blonde tresses would be plaited and coiled at the base of her neck.

Finally the dress was finished, and Shasta, accompanied by several of the faeries, was taken to a guest toadstool to be dressed and to have her hair attended to. Meanwhile Abelia had taken May to her toadstool to talk.

"Well, May, you are aware that Merlin is here, of course, and in human form? She said.

"Yes I 'saw' him. So history will repeat itself," she said softly.

"Exactly my words," said Abelia.

"Maybe it is for the best," said May.

"Issues need resolving, but they are both young and Shasta's powers will be demonstrated soon I feel. The village will greatly benefit, for I have spoken."

"I would love to see a happy ending for them," said May

Moving on, Abelia said, "It's beginning to get light now and it's time for you to be getting back to the cottage. Let's see how Shasta is getting on with my faeries."

Walking back companionably to the guest toadstool, they put their heads inside to look at Shasta. May and Abelia both gasped in amazement. She looked absolutely radiant now that she was dressed and her hair was finished. Her skin was a golden brown from the time spent in the garden and her blonde hair, entwined with forget me knots and Shasta daisies, gleamed and shone. The dress fitted her like a second skin and was finished off by the shoes of silver and blue which sparked with faery dust. Every time Shasta moved, a cloud of rainbow coloured faery dust rose around her.

"Oh, my lovely, you look so beautiful you almost bring me to tears."

Rushing over to May, Shasta pulled her into an embrace.

"Please don't be upset, May. I'm so pleased that you like how I look. If only Merlin were here to see me."

Suddenly the faeries surrounding her began to titter in amusement.

"Enough, faeries," ordered Abelia, clapping her hands in the form of dismissal, anxious not to spoil the surprise. "Leave us."

"Yes, your majesty," they said.

Abelia, a woman of few words said, "Shasta, my dear, you will make any man proud of you but now is the time to go back to the cottage."

"You are right, Abelia. Come, Shasta, let us return," said May.

Chapter 14

May and Shasta were back in the garden. Having drunk from the well, they were now normal size.

"Every year on Shasta Day, I perform a ritual to Nertha [Mother Earth] for good crops and harvests for the villagers," said May.

"Does it work for flowers as well, Aunt?" Shasta asked.

"Oh yes, my dear, that's why I perform the ritual in my garden, but it is for the good of all," she said. "As soon as I take this phone call I will do it."

No sooner had the words left May's mouth, than the phone began to ring.

How strange, thought Shasta, she hadn't thought about her parents at all, and they would be the only ones to phone May. Most villagers had phones but they didn't seem to bother with them much as they saw each other almost daily.

As this thought entered her head, she heard her aunt say. "Hello, Iris, how are things with you and George in Holland? Oh, dear, I'm sorry to hear that. Yes, she's sitting in the garden. I'll go and get her for you."

Hearing this, Shasta came in and took the phone from her aunt.

"Hello, Mother," she said. "How are you and father coping in Holland?"

"Summer, is that you? No it can't be, you sound so different. Can you please put my daughter on the phone? George there is someone on the phone saying she's Summer and she sounds nothing like her. Whatever is my sister playing at? What has she done to my little girl? Will you please put my daughter on the phone? George, why did you suggest leaving our only daughter with my eccentric sister? You should have known better."

This all came from her mother in one breath. Shasta didn't know whether to laugh or be exasperated.

She decided that she would pretend to be one of her aunt's friends playing a joke. Wait... this was Shasta the village of magic. She could change her voice back to Summer's. Her mother wouldn't be any the wiser.

So she said, "Hello, Mummy, did you like my impression of a grown-up?"

"Hello, Summer darling, you really frightened me. I wasn't sure what had happened to you. Are you all right there with Aunt May?"

"Yes, thank you. We're getting on very well. We shop in the village and I am learning the names of the flowers. Daddy will be very proud of me, I think."

"Summer, things are quite terrible out here and your father and I would like to stay on for a while. Would that be alright with you? Please tell me if it isn't, won't you?"

Shasta found it difficult to contain her excitement. The thought of staying on in Shasta was a joy beyond belief.

"I really don't mind, Mummy, there's plenty for me to do here. Have you asked Aunt May yet?"

"Yes. She doesn't mind at all. I will phone you again soon, then. Bye, darling."

"Bye, Mummy," said Shasta.

Shasta was beside herself with glee. She couldn't believe her luck. Extra time in Shasta with Aunt May and her beloved Merlin who still hadn't returned, although she had felt his presence about.

"Oh, Aunt May, I feel sorry for my parents and their problems in Holland but it will be wonderful to have more time in Shasta," She said.

"It was meant to be, my mistress. Come, let's talk to Nertha, but first we will cleanse our hands." said May.

So going to the sink they both washed their hands thoroughly, Shasta taking care not to spoil her dress. With Shasta beside her, May lifted her arms up to the skies and spoke the incantation of the ritual to Nertha.

Bowing her head she stood for a moment or two, and then said, "Well, my lovely, I will now change into my clothes for the fair and we'll walk to the village."

"Oh yes," said Shasta.

"I'll wait here on the swing seat for you."

As Shasta sat waiting for May, she began to feel quite guilty because she hadn't missed her parents. She loved them both dearly, although her mother had some funny ways at times. She now knew that she belonged here with May and Merlin. 'Beloved Merlin, I wonder where you are. Yet I don't feel any harm has become you....' *Strange*, she thought, *I sound like my history books at school.*

Somehow she didn't feel she would be going back to school next term, or ever again for that matter.

Chapter 15

May had changed into the dress she planned to wear and was now making a decision as to whether to wear her hair loose or in her usual plait. She decided to ask Shasta's opinion. As she walked through to the garden, she was aware of Shasta being deep in thought. Well, everything would be resolved over the next two days, she thought to herself.

"Shasta, can I please ask your..."

".....Why, Aunt, you look absolutely beautiful," said Shasta stopping May in mid sentence. "That colour and style really looks wonderful on you. All of the men will be longing to dance with you."

"Well thank you for your confidence in me," May said. "I came out to ask if you think I should wear my hair loose or in my usual plait."

"Oh, Aunt, can I do your hair for you, please? We can weave some flowers into it as well."

May just laughed, caught up in her enthusiasm. "Lets go back to my bedroom," she said, "and you can style it in front of the mirror."

May sat down in front of the mirror while Shasta loosened her aunt's plait. The hair seemed to almost reach the ground. Shasta had expected it to be heavy in texture, but instead it was light and silky smooth. On a whim she decided to do it exactly the same as her own. Instead of having two plaits coiled in the nape of the neck, she made several. The style made her aunt look even younger. The finishing touch would be to weave flowers into it, but what to choose and what colours? Her aunt's dress was maroon velvet cut very deep at the back and front and edged with fine fur. The sleeves were gathered just above the elbows and fell away to be edged with cream lace. The waist of the dress fell into a v-shape from the hips and flowed to her feet. On her feet were soft maroon slippers with a small heel the same as Shasta's.

Impulsively she tried out her powers. She imagined purple and red fuchsias in her aunts' hair, woven in and around the neck. Instantly the flowers appeared but didn't look right. *I have it,* thought Shasta. She had remembered a cream coloured fuchsia in her aunt's garden. The outer petals were edged with pale lilac, while the inner petals were pale cream like marshmallow, the stamens a very pale red colour. Instantly the whole effect was changed. Showing the hair from all angles with the use of mirrors and looking at her aunt's face, she knew she had achieved the desired effect.

May just sat looking at herself. In her mind she was remembering her own youth and how she felt. *Who knows what will happen in the next two days,* she thought, with a little bit of excitement. Giving herself a mental ticking off for being a silly old woman and not acting her age, she thanked Shasta for all the effort, and now they must get to the village. The villagers would not start anything until Shasta's arrival.

As they approached the village green, the sight that met her overwhelmed Shasta. Everyone seemed to be dressed in different styles and costumes. Some of the men wore smocks and breeches. The smocks almost came to their knees and the breeches were tied at the knees or ankles. They had black hats on their heads with wide brims. Others wore doublets with embroidered shirts underneath, and tights. The maidens wore either a frock with an apron on top, or shawls instead of aprons. On their head they wore either a white mobcap or straw hats which were covered in flowers. This, explained May, was quite normal. It allowed people to let their imagination explore different eras just for the day, or two days in this case. As she moved to the centre of the green, there was a reverential hush. Many of the men once again tugged at their forelocks and the women bobbed down. Some were afraid to look at Shasta; she seemed to be transformed. Her magnificent clothes were totally worthy of her status. She put her hand out to each of them as she passed by, feeling very close to all of them.

Turning round she held her arms aloft as before. "People of Shasta, once again this day is upon us. There is food in abundance, ale to be drunk by the barrel, sports games to be played by the energetic, and music to be danced to. So, Morris dancers, take up the ribbons of the tree and start the dancing."

As Shasta said this, the six Morris dancers bedecked in white, and with flowers and ribbons attached to their hats, began to dance. The intricate pattern of the coloured ribbons around the may tree were gradually being woven into a long plait until they reached the bottom. Other Morris dancers in groups of six, with bells on their shoes, did traditional dances with wooden staves which were knocked together at regular intervals. At a far corner of the green, two roasting spits were set up to roast the bulls and rams. Some of the children were chasing a pig around trying to catch it, mostly for the fun of it and not as a means of sustenance. Others walked about peddling their wares.

"Buy my pretty ribbons, my friends, and give to your wives and lady loves," they chorused.

The music was infectious and maidens and young men were dancing to the many fiddles being played. Girls with garlands in their hair were being treated to ribbons to hang from them, a sign of undying love from the men. Another part of the green was set aside for sporting fixtures. Men were stripped to the waist wrestling each other while maidens raced up and down the green for prizes, knowing that occasionally the prize was just a kiss from a stranger, causing much ribald laughter. Out of harm's way, men were throwing javelins, casting stones and running the sack race, mostly falling over but righting themselves again much to the fun of the onlookers cheering them on. Children were encouraged to take their chances on the greasy pole, knocking their opponent off with a feather pillow. As the evening got cooler, the giant bonfire would be lit to ensure warmth for all who wanted it.

Shasta watched all this and was encouraged to join in the games and judge the winners of others. Good naturedly she made the best of it all by dancing with some of the men and ensuring that May joined in also. On one occasion, laughingly, she insisted that her aunt accepted a love token of a ribbon from a rather handsome local man who had set his cap on her. May was secretly flattered by this but kept him at a distance.

Even though she was enjoying herself, Shasta felt lonely. She had hoped Merlin would turn up at the cottage just to let her know that he was around, but since he had disappeared no one had seen him.

Chapter 16

Merlin had been watching Shasta and May from just inside the guest toadstool. If he stood to the side of the entrance, he was hidden from view but still able to see what was going on. He had seen Shasta leave the kingdom with the faeries. She had looked so beautiful; he just wanted to touch her face and tell her so. At the same time, he was frightened and overwhelmed by her beauty. What chance would he have, he wondered, full of self-doubt. It had taken every bit of his will power not to reveal himself to her. He also sought her approval of his human form. How would she react, he wondered. Would he be pleasing to her eye? He hadn't seen what he looked like and he hoped Shasta would love him as much now as she did in their previous life.

With all these thoughts going through his mind, he was still reluctant to leave the safety of the kingdom for fear of rejection from Shasta. Perhaps he had misunderstood her feelings for him when he was a cat.

Abelia sat on her lavender throne watching the faeries at their work around the kingdom. After the excitement of Merlin becoming human and hiding him while they were dressing Shasta, things had gone back to normal and everything seemed very quiet now. Her two princesses, Jasmine and Day Lilly, sat on either side of her while Evening Primrose bossed the other faeries about as usual. None of them really minded as they were happy to serve the Queen through her. Abelia had told them on one occasion when she wasn't around that she was all bark with no bite which encouraged the faeries to view her quite differently.

They all had different jobs according to their rank in the kingdom. Some had to ensure there was enough pollen for the bees to collect for their honey. Others had to ensure that all the flowers had enough sun shining on them so they could grow healthily.

Occasionally a fern had to be gently pulled up and planted elsewhere, or pushed aside, to let the early rays of the morning sun through. Silkworms and spiders had to have enough room to do their spinning. The silk from the worms was sometimes used by the faeries to lie over the delicate flowers at night to keep them warm if need be. As the gentle night rain fell on the silk it, gave the impression of many shimmering prisms. Other faeries had to ensure that money was left under children's pillows when their milk teeth had fallen out.

As Abelia sat watching, her thoughts turned to Merlin. Glancing at him sitting amidst the moss and bark on the ground, she couldn't understand why he was looking so sad. He should be ecstatic with happiness. Using her powers to read his mind, she soon realised his problem. He was unsure of Shasta's feelings for him. She was very much in love with Merlin but he needed a lot of convincing. He was such a handsome man all of the maidens would be interested in him.

Bending over to Jasmine, Abelia asked her to bring Merlin to her.

"Yes, your Majesty," she said.

Going over to Merlin she invited him to come and talk with the Queen.

"Very well, Jasmine," he said.

Following Jasmine he walked over and bent on one knee to Abelia, at the same time taking off his cap and bowing his head in an exaggerated fashion.

"I see you are as cheeky as ever, young Merlin. If you wish to pay homage to me, please do it in the time honoured fashion and not this flamboyant style you have adopted of late," she said trying to keep the humour from her voice.

"Please forgive me, your Majesty, I meant no disrespect." With that he bowed to Abelia as decorum dictated.

"That's better, Merlin," she admonished.

"Princesses Jasmine and Day Lily, will you please leave us? I wish to talk to Merlin alone."

"Yes, your Majesty," they said and, rising, they walked off to a discreet distance away.

"Merlin, it seems to me you have the troubles of everyone on your shoulders. I thought you were happy to be human again," she said gently.

"Oh, Abelia, I'm so happy to be human again and for everything you have done for me. I'm just so frightened that when I see Shasta she will be disappointed in how I look as a human."

"Any maiden with a sane mind would be excited by the way you look, Merlin."

Instantly, she regretted letting her thoughts escape through her mouth. She was the Queen and above such things. It was too late, though. Slowly a smile spread around Merlin's mouth, he raised one eyebrow questioningly and his eyes began to sparkle.

"So you think I'm a fine catch, my Queen," he said.

"Merlin, remember your place," she said but her statement lacked the usual authority. "I would strongly suggest you go to the fair and claim Shasta. She loved you in her past life, I'm sure her feelings will not have changed in this one."

Rising to his feet, Merlin took off his cap and made a broad sweep of the ground with it, bowing low as he did so. Then he left to join the villagers at the fair.

As Merlin left, Abelia felt that everything around her suddenly seemed quite empty.

"Oh well," she said half to herself.

Clapping her hands she summoned her princesses back to enable them to report how the day was progressing.

Chapter 17

Merlin left the faery kingdom with a light heart. The sun was setting as he walked towards the village and he whistled to himself contentedly. Nearing the green he began to get caught up in the enthusiasm of all the activities. Close by men were wrestling.

"Would you care to take on the winner, young sir?" called out one man in a smock and breeches.

"I don't think so, thank you," Merlin replied with a laugh.

Many of the maidens approached him shyly but, although friendly, he was uninterested. As a peddler went by selling his wares, Merlin purchased a blue and white ribbon which he intended to present to Shasta as a love token.

"Good luck, sir, I'm sure the young lady will be only too pleased to accept it".

"I hope you're right," he said with an earnest expression.

Merlin decided to walk over to the far edge of the green and watch for Shasta from there. Maybe he would see May also. As it was getting dark, it was more difficult to see.

May sensed that Merlin was here but couldn't see him yet. She had finally broken free from the man who had given her the love token ribbon. Given different circumstances, she may well have been interested, but her first priority was to watch over Shasta and look out for Merlin.

He was here, she could feel it in her bones, but where?

Many of the villagers had settled round the giant bonfire. It was always lit on Shasta Day to confer health and prosperity on the community. Children lay comfortably up against their mothers whilst the men sang quietly, lulling the children to the land of dreams. Others were eating and drinking whilst at the same time enjoying the fierce heat of the fire.

May saw Shasta in the distance, still looking as beautiful as when they arrived. She was talking to a group of farmers.

As May went to approach her, a voice in her ear said, "Hello, May, how are you?" May span round with excitement and almost lost her footing as she saw Merlin before her.

The vision she had seen in Faery Cove was as nothing compared to the real thing. Merlin looked so much more handsome in the flesh, more refined and distinguished than in his previous human life. *Oh, my dearest Merlin,* thought May, *you look wonderful*.

Seeing his concerned face, May said out loud, "Fear not, Merlin, all will be well, I promise you."

Merlin's face relaxed slightly. "Where is Shasta, my mistress? I can't wait any longer."

"Over yonder," May said using the olde words which seemed to fit the occasion. Merlin looked to where she pointed and his heart lifted. Shasta stood talking to a group of local villagers. As he moved towards them, the crowd parted. With some of them it was simply out of recognition and with others it was out of awe. The conversation around Shasta stopped suddenly and she was at a loss as to why. They had been talking about the harvest that had just been brought in. One by one they drifted away. For a moment she didn't understand and was about to say so.

"Oh my beloved Shasta, my mistress, you are so beautiful, I feel my heart will burst with love."

Shasta stood still, unable to move. The voices in her head were telling her it was Merlin and that he was human, but sometimes she found it hard to come to terms with the gift of clairvoyance. Plucking up courage, she turned round and almost swooned. Merlin took two steps backwards and, doffing his cap, he swept it to the ground and bowed to his mistress. In kind, Shasta did a deep curtsey. Merlin's dark blue costume complimented Shasta' sky-blue dress and it was agreed they made a handsome couple. Standing upright, he replaced his hat and took hold of both of her hands in his. Gently kissing each one in turn, he pulled her towards him and finally kissed her mouth. As her looked into her eyes, he read there all he wanted to know.

All around them the villagers stood in awe. Those that knew the story of Merlin and Shasta explained in hushed whispers to those who weren't sure of all the details. Everywhere the sound of "Ah" could be heard. With understanding, they were left alone; after all it was two hundred years ago that Shasta had last met him in human form. Shasta looked at Merlin with longing, unable to believe how incredibly handsome he was, while Merlin looked at Shasta and couldn't believe her extraordinary beauty. May watched from afar with tears in her eyes.

At last, my mistress, she thought to herself, *you have what you wanted most. Don't let him go, for it's in your hands to change history, choose wisely for the happiness of all.*

May went and sat by the fire, suddenly feeling very alone.

"So there you are, May," said a voice close by.

"I have been looking everywhere for you. Shall we take a quiet walk?"

It was the handsome local man she had met earlier.

"Why not?" she said,

"First, though, tell me your name," she asked.

"Erasmus," he said with a secretive smile.

"I like that name very much. Yes, it is a beautiful evening and the rain has just started to fall, why not?" said May.

"I love to walk in the rain," said Erasmus. "It's very refreshing, don't you think?"

"I agree," said May with a hint of laughter and, fingering the love ribbon he had given her, she linked her arm in his.

Chapter 18

As they walked slowly away from the villagers, Merlin declared his love for Shasta by giving her the blue and white ribbon he had purchased earlier. He threaded it into the plaited coil at the nape of her neck. As with a lovers knot, their own love was sealed forever. Holding both her hands in front of him, he had never been so happy and told Shasta so while she declared her love for him. Her only concern was how long he would be human but she was reluctant to mention this to him. At the same time Merlin was asking himself the same question.

As they walked to the edge of the village green by the field, they noticed some hayricks. At various intervals, couples were dotted about in lovers' embraces.

In mutual agreement Shasta and Merlin decided to sit down. In reverence to Shasta, the other couples moved away one by one, leaving them on their own. Wrapped in each other's arms, and emotionally exhausted, they fell asleep.

The following morning, as Shasta awoke, she felt a heavy weight on her waist. With excitement she realised it was Merlin's arm. So she hadn't dreamt it after all. She lay still prolonging the moment for as long as possible. Merlin was experiencing a similar dream, firstly that he was human and secondly that he had his arm around his beloved mistress, Shasta. Opening his eyes he savoured her beauty, with the realisation that it wasn't a dream after all. As he did this Shasta opened her eyes and they just absorbed one another.

"Oh, my beautiful Shasta, let this moment never pass," he said to her.

"I have never stopped loving you, Merlin".

"My Shasta, your beauty has spanned two lifetimes," he said as tears welled in his eyes.

"Please don't cry, my beloved. This is a happy moment for both of us."

Sitting up, she suddenly became serious. "I have to ensure that you will always stay in human form," she said. "I need to ask Abelia's advice, Merlin. Can you bear to be parted from me while I do this?"

"I don't wish to be parted from you for one minute, but I will go back to May's cottage and wait for you".

Kissing both of her upturned palms, he bid her a temporary farewell and made his way back to the cottage, instantly feeling lonely. Shasta sat quietly for a moment trying to collect her thoughts. He was so handsome her heart pounded in her chest. Could it really be three lifetimes ago that she had last touched him as a human? It seemed almost impossible to take in. She needed to see Abelia straightaway. As she thought it, she was suddenly in the faery kingdom. Taken by surprise, and still wearing the same clothes, she was reduced in size again, her clothes shrinking in the same proportion.

She stood before Abelia and the princesses Jasmine and Day Lily.

"Shasta, my dear, how can I help you?"

"Abelia, I have to be sure that Merlin will never change from human form again to ensure our continued happiness," she said. "But I am unsure what to do."

"My dear Shasta, this is your village and you seem to have forgotten that you have the power to change the past and the present as you see fit."

"Yes, of course, why do I keep forgetting that? I'm just not used to it yet, Abelia, and I'm so frightened of losing Merlin again. I will do anything to keep him human. I will take a walk and think about what must be done."

"Very well, my dear, but remember I have no power to change anything. That is your prerogative alone but I will be here if you need advice," she said.

Shasta paced endlessly, wondering what to do for the best. This power was all new to her. She understood that it could only be used for the good of all and that she must use it wisely. Dealing with an affair of the heart, was that using it wisely, she questioned herself. Suddenly a complete calm came over her. "Of course, why didn't I think of that before?"

Rushing back to Abelia, she needed to confirm her own doubts as to whether it was possible.

Abelia had been sitting patiently waiting for Shasta, knowing she would in time come to the right decision. Finally that moment had arrived and Shasta came rushing towards her, tripping over the hem of her dress in her haste. Righting herself, she threw herself at Abelia's feet.

"Oh, Abelia," she said in excitement, "I have the solution to the problem."

"And you wish me to confirm if it is possible," said Abelia.

"Abelia, you knew what I was thinking," Shasta said.

"Of course, my dear, that is why I am Queen of the faeries, and everything will come to pass providing the intention is good."

Shasta immediately thought of Merlin and May and the cottage, and she was back in the garden. As she walked towards the swing seat, she saw Merlin and May deep in conversation. He was so handsome. At that moment Merlin caught sight of her. He was instantly up and at her side.

"My beloved Shasta, I've missed you."

"It was only a couple of hours, Merlin."

"Two hours too long," he said.

May stood to go inside, believing she wasn't needed at this moment.

"No, May, please stay as this concerns you too," Shasta said, observing that May's face seemed very radiant. Then she noticed the love token of ribbons in May's hair, but decided not to comment.

"You have made a decision then, my mistress?" asked May, a bit concerned.

"Yes," she said. "I will tell you on the way to the village. I think it's time we started to enjoy the last day of the fair."

As the three of them walked through the front gate of the cottage, Shasta walked in the middle and linked her arms through Merlin's on the right and May's on the left. Strolling towards the village green, Shasta revealed her plan which was completely possible as she was Shasta in every sense of the word. As they neared the green, the villagers were already enjoying themselves. A bull was being roasted on one of the spits and a ram on the other. Children were running everywhere and laughing, and stopping to look shyly at Shasta as she walked past with Merlin. May, on the pretext of leaving them alone together, walked off to see if she could see her friend Erasmus from the night before. She hoped that he would notice that she now wore the love token in her hair. Thinking about what Shasta had told her, she now felt more relaxed. Yes, she thought to herself, that would be the safest way to right the wrong in their young lives. Suddenly she heard raised voices and a cheer. Looking to the middle of the green, she could see the beginning of a procession. Hurrying over to join in, she watched an arbour of flowers being held aloft by four men, two supporting the front and two at the back. It was being held over Shasta and Merlin. This was an old tradition performed by the villagers to recognise Shasta as their own Queen. Merlin, enjoying himself immensely, had hold of Shasta's right hand, with his other hand on his hip as if ready to dance the minuet. In this fashion they walked in honour around the edge of the green, protected from the sun by the arbour of flowers carried by the bearers. As they passed by the groups of people, there was much cheering and laughing. Having reached their starting point they broke free of the arbour. The music from the fiddles began and Merlin bowed low to Shasta to ask for the pleasure of dancing with her. Curtseying low, she agreed. As they danced together, the villagers watched in appreciation, marvelling at how well they suited one another. They all quietly agreed it would be a tragedy if Merlin were ever to revert to being a cat again. As May looked on at them dancing, she was aware of someone behind her.

"They dance well, the young couple. Should we show them how it should be done, May?"

As May turned to say she thought she was getting too old to dance and cavort about, she was swept up by Erasmus to dance alongside Merlin and Shasta. After a few moments the other villagers joined in. The dancing went on for a couple of hours with couples joining in and then dropping out for food or refreshment as the mood took them.

May and Erasmus stayed dancing for almost as long as Merlin and Shasta, but eventually May had to concede defeat due to thirst and fatigue, even though she was content to be held indefinitely by Erasmus. This feeling of love in the air was infectious, she thought to herself. As the sun began to set and the bonfire was lit once more, Shasta raised her hands for silence.

"People of Shasta," she said, "we have had two days of festivities. Many love trysts have been made and kept."

As she said this she looked in May's direction and felt happiness in her heart for May and Erasmus.

"I now have to right a wrong, which happened many years ago. I know that I will be successful because it is for the good of all the village of Shasta, and also for me." With this her face softened as she looked towards Merlin. "The festivities should go on until the bewitching hour and then you should return to your homes."

With this she dropped her hands to her side and walked towards Merlin. With a brief look at May and Erasmus, she joined hands with Merlin and they began to blend with the night sky, leaving a thin trail of smoke where they had been. Shasta and Merlin were now in their past with whatever it might bring forth.

Chapter 19

May had started to walk back towards her cottage with Erasmus, but now stopped to consult him. What was her sister going to say, she wondered?

Iris and George had left their only daughter, Summer, who was merely eight and three-quarters, in her charge. In three weeks she had not only turned the child's hair from red to blonde, which admittedly had been for her own good, but she had also changed her into a mature young woman, and she had introduced her to a faery Queen who lived in a cove at the bottom of her garden.

On top of all this, May had to explain that not only was she not Summer Backer as she thought herself to be, but Shasta of Shasta village where she was now living. In a previous life she had fallen in love with a young man, who had become a cat and come to live with May in this life, waiting for Shasta to return. Shasta had fallen in love with him over again, even though he was still a cat. He had returned to human form and now Shasta and he had gone back in time to right the wrong and ensure that he stayed human in this life.

"No wonder my sister calls me eccentric," she said out loud to Erasmus. "I do believe I might be."

Erasmus just smiled, linked arms with May and they carried on walking.

Book 2:

Shasta Village

Chapter 20

The present

"Are you drunk, May?"

"Certainly not, Iris, I've never been drunk in my life. Well, except when you married George and that was only because I felt sorry for him."

George started to laugh but choked on the sweet he had been eating.

In her early forties, and older than his wife, his sister-in-law was really comical at times. Iris continued with her tirade ignoring their derision.

"I leave our daughter in your charge, May, for three weeks while George and I are in Holland on business and now you tell me she is no longer here at the cottage, that she is now called Shasta and that she has fallen in love with a cat that was originally a boy she met in a previous life. On top of all that, she has now apparently gone back two hundred years to her past life with him to right a wrong and, if I understood you correctly, you have faeries living in the bottom of your garden. You tell me this is a magical village, but I was right, May, you really are eccentric and I said so to George when we left Summer here. Yes, Summer! The name we christened her with. George, don't just sit there, do something, anything! I'm going to have an attack of the vapours."

As usual, her husband had sat calmly and quietly listening to his wife's outrage, but taking in all May was saying.

"Iris, this is the twenty-first century and women do not have attacks of the vapours anymore, they go to see analysts. As I have no intention of paying for one, just sit and listen to what May is saying, even though I agree it is a shock," George replied.

"Iris, can I get you a cup of camomile tea to help calm you," asked

May.

"No, I'll have a cup of Earl Grey in a bone china cup, if you please, May. I'm in shock and George said so."

"What can I get you, George?"

"Anything will be fine, thank you, May," he said.

May left them in the sitting room of her cottage discussing the news she had just imparted. Passing the two bedrooms and the bathroom, she made her way into the kitchen. How she missed Merlin and her mistress, Shasta. Yes she could visit Faery Cove for company, but it wasn't the same as having them around.

Oh well, she thought, *I knew it wasn't going to be easy explaining to my sister. She is so highly strung these days. It must be the pressure of the problems within the garden centre.*

George Backer owned two garden centres, one in England and one in Holland. The Dutch one was run by Henney, their manager. In a phone call from Henney, George had learnt that their centre had been vandalised and the Dutch Police had charged no-one as yet. They had been there for three weeks while their daughter had been staying with May.

"Are you making that tea, May?" called her sister from the sitting room.

"I'm just coming."

"Right," thought May, "I'll have camomile tea, Earl Grey for Iris, and George can have Indian."

As she imagined the tea in her mind, it appeared before her on the table. Putting it on a tray, she carried it back into the sitting room. She may be getting a bit long in the tooth but her powers were still there.

Iris started on her tea straightaway.

"Excellent cup of tea, May. How is yours, George?" Iris asked

"May always makes a smashing cup of tea."

He and May had something of a soft spot for one another.

"I feel better already," said Iris.

She was starting to relax now into the back of the large chintz-covered sofa which stood to the side of the open fireplace. George sat opposite her in the other matching two-seater settee, while May favoured her rocking chair piled with cushions. Set out this way, it made for easy conversations.

There had been a beautiful evening sunset but May had now drawn the heavy chintz curtains across the windows as the night had drawn in. When Merlin and Shasta were here, they mostly left the curtains open to enjoy the moonlight. It wasn't cold enough to light a fire yet as it was only September but there was a cosy atmosphere, if she said so herself.

"I have to admit there's something about this cottage and the village, May. They have a relaxing influence on me. Maybe it's the sun; it always seems to shine here through the whole of the summer months. Even in the winter it never seems cold or unpleasant," Iris said. "There's no order to the garden, unlike ours at home, but the flowers look so beautiful and always seem so vibrant and alive."

May just smiled to herself. Having imparted the information about her niece, how could she tell her sister that Shasta was a magic village steeped in history and legends? Iris' only daughter, Summer, as she had christened her, was in fact called Shasta and the village was named after her.

When Summer had turned up at her aunt's, May had told her, over her three weeks stay, the history of her previous life with Merlin She had also told her about Faery Cove which was situated through the gate at the bottom of May's garden. During the course of those weeks, Summer-Shasta had also met Abelia, the faery queen, who had reinforced May's words to her. Shasta had the power to change the past. During this time the villagers had come to recognise that she was indeed Shasta from the past reincarnated in this lifetime.

The power of love between Shasta and Merlin had finally overcome the spell that had turned Merlin into a cat, and Merlin had returned to human form. In an effort to ensure that Merlin stayed permanently human, they had gone back to their previous life of two hundred years ago to rectify the situation and, in effect, change history. It was a dangerous journey to embark upon but, furnished with Shasta's powers, it was possible.

Breaking into her thoughts, George said,

"Well, there is nothing more that we can do tonight, Iris. I suggest we unpack our cases and retire for the night."

Yawning several times, Iris was already beginning to doze.

"I agree, George. Although it's only nine o'clock, I'm finding it hard to keep my eyes open. I bid you goodnight then, May, and we'll see you in the morning."

As the words left her mouth, Iris thought what a strange way that was to say goodnight.

Normally she would just say 'Goodnight, May' and retire. Nothing much seemed to surprise her anymore, though. Her sister seemed to have a strange influence over her in a nice sort of way. She made up her mind to visit May more often in the future. Shasta Village was beginning to grow on her. George followed Iris into the bedroom and started to unpack the cases whilst Iris lay on the bed half propped up by the pillows and her elbows.

Looking around the room, she took in the patchwork quilt on the bed and the matching curtains. In one corner there was a wardrobe and the two chests of drawers sat one on each side of the bed. In the opposite corner was a wicker chair with cushions which also matched the curtains.

Iris decided the room definitely had cosy feel and she was sure she would sleep well. Knowing that her daughter had also slept in the room was especially comforting to her. The mattress on the bed seemed to mould itself around her body and she was having trouble staying awake.

George put the last of their clothes into the drawers and, as he turned around to take the case off of the bed, he realised that Iris was virtually asleep.

"Come on, Iris, let me help you get undressed and into bed. I didn't realise you were that tired."

Fortunately she wasn't very heavy and George was able to pull her upright, albeit in a rather undignified way. Seemingly unable to help, Iris just seemed to flop about. Eventually George managed to get her out of her clothes and into a nightie, and then into bed, where she promptly fell asleep. Realising he wasn't as tired as he first thought, he wandered back out towards the kitchen where he noticed that the back door was open and headed towards it. Stepping outside, he found May sitting in the two-seater swing seat.

"Can I join you, May?" he asked.

"I'd be pleased of the company." She patted the vacant seat beside her.

George sat down and they stayed that way for a few moments in a companionable silence, both watching the moon and the shadows it cast around the garden.

"Iris is asleep, then?" enquired May.

"Yes, I have never known her to fall asleep so quickly. It's a blessed relief, if I'm honest."

"Tiredness creeps up on you in Shasta when you aren't used to the country air," she said.

With that the gentle rain began to fall, and the plants and the earth drank greedily.

The strangest thing of all was not only didn't George feel cold but also he wasn't getting wet.

"Shasta is a very special village. Sometimes you just have to accept everything that happens around you without question."

"Yes, but ... "

"Hush, just take my word for it, my dear. I promise no harm will come to you in Shasta. You have my word on that."

As he wondered silently what on earth was happening around him, he also questioned his sanity, although he had to admit to himself that he felt very relaxed about the whole situation.

"You know, May, for the first time in a long time I feel absolutely relaxed and in need of a beer."

"But you rarely drink, George. Are you sure?" May replied.

"Absolutely" he said with conviction.

Oh well, thought May, *here goes,* and immediately two bottles of beer appeared in her hands.

"Good God, May!!..... How? ... What? .... "

"Oh, it's just magic George, pure magic."

"But how? ... [then] .... I wonder if we could bottle it, May?" he said and they both laughed at his joke.

As they drank their beers straight from the bottle, George began to question everything that had happened. He could listen to May properly now without Iris around him getting stressed.

"Well, as I tried to explain earlier, Shasta village has a magical quality. That is something you either accept or you don't. Most people in my experience have faired much better if they accept it. The rain, for instance, only happens at night, regardless of the season. Flowers also come into bloom here out of season. If you wish something to bloom, it will. During the summer months the sun shines for hours on end. That was one of the reasons I changed your daughter's hair to blonde. Her red hair was causing her to burn terribly and I don't think you will be disappointed when you see how mature she has become."

"How mature has she become, May?" George asked, rather concerned. "She was eight and three quarters when we left her here."

"You will have to accept the fact that, because of overriding events that have happened in Shasta, she has grown into a young woman and she has now aged to at least eighteen years since being here, George. But she is absolutely beautiful. Shasta is her heritage. I knew from the day she was born when I visited the hospital that she was the legendary Shasta reincarnated. I could see it in her eyes. I also knew that one day she would return and remember all that had happened in the past. It was only a matter of time before everything came back to her, with a little prompting from Abelia and me, of course."

"Who is Abelia?" George asked.

"The faery Queen, George."

"The faery Que... oh give me a break, May, this is George you're talking to. I'm forty-six years old and I stopped thinking about the tooth faery and Father Christmas many years ago."

"Well, I think you're going to be in need of a rethink on that score, George."

"So where are these faeries, then and can I have another beer, please, May?" As he said it, so another full bottle appeared in his hand.

"Well, I'll be ... "

"Be careful what you ask for, George - you may get a surprise."

"So I see," he said with amusement He rather liked it here in Shasta.

"As I was saying, May, where are these faeries, then?"

"At the bottom of my garden, George. Faeries mostly live at the bottom of the garden. I thought you, as a market gardener, would know that."

"If I started to talk to the public about faeries at the bottom of a garden, I would either go broke or end up a millionaire with the publicity."

"Well, these faeries only appear at night and they live at the very bottom of the garden through the gate by the wishing well." All this was said with emphasis, to get the point across.

"Don't tell me. To get into the faery kingdom you have to drink from the wishing well and shrink in size so that you don't frighten them," George said smugly.

"How did you know that, George?" May asked feigning surprise.

"You're kidding, you mean you really have to do that? I was

making it up as I went along, May," George said incredulously.

"How would you feel if you came upon a giant, George. Wouldn't you feel rather frightened?"

"Realistically, I suppose I would – yes," he said thoughtfully. "Hey, wait a minute, you are making all this up aren't you? I know your sense of humour, May," he teased her, half hoping that he was right and half hoping that maybe faeries did exist at the bottom of May's garden. What a story that would make.

"Actually I thought you of all people would believe I was telling you the truth, George."

"It really is true, then, all of it?"

"I'm afraid so, George," said May with some feeling, wishing to reassure him once and for all.

"In that case, let's get another round in and this time make it doubles," George said. No sooner was the remark out of his mouth, instantly four bottles of beer appeared at his feet which caused them both to laugh out loud.

When they had finished their drinks, George decided to head for bed and sleep on all that May had told him.

How was he going to convince Iris that May wasn't mad or eccentric, and that not only was their daughter going on eighteen, but she had grown to a young woman and had magical powers that she was apparently born with.

By the time he had finished explaining, he would probably need an analyst, and his wife would need one too.

Chapter 21

The following morning Iris woke first, while George lay on his back gently snoring beside her. Strange that, he normally only snored when he had been drinking. Oh well, she thought to herself, that means I can savour this moment before he wakes up. Stretching her body with a feeling of sensuousness, she snuggled down again. Oh this bed and mattress were so comfortable; they seemed to hug themselves around her body. They really were quite sensuous. *Iris Baker, what are you thinking of?* she admonished herself.

She began to try and make sense of everything her sister had told her about Summer, or should she call her Shasta now while she was here. It was all so confusing to her. George seemed to take everything in his stride.

As she thought this, he suddenly let out a long exaggerated snort and woke up. Turning to Iris he asked if she had had a good sleep.

"Yes, thank you, George, I can't remember when I last slept so well, I must admit. This bed is so comfy. Did you know you were snoring, by the way?"

"After you went to sleep, I went back out to the garden, and May and I had a couple of beers before I came back to bed."

"Whatever possessed you, George, you rarely drink."

"Well, under the circumstances I felt it was justified, Iris. It isn't every day you find out that your daughter was alive two hundred years ago and that she has magical powers."

"What are we going to do, George?"

"Well, there is nothing much that we can do at the moment, so I'm going to get up and make a cup of coffee. Would you like a cup of tea, Iris?"

"Yes please, George, that would be lovely. I must admit I am quite reluctant to leave this bed."

"Stay here, then. I'll bring it to you when it's made."

Putting on his dressing gown and slippers, George padded out to the kitchen. May was already at the table drinking coffee and eating toast.

"Morning, May. It's a lovely morning again. Iris is lying in this morning courtesy of your comfy bed. Thought I would give her tea in bed. Where's the teapot?"

May laughed. "Remember our conversation last night, George? I don't actually possess a teapot. This is Shasta, remember?" If you just think about a cup of Earl Grey in a bone china cup, it will appear for you."

"So it wasn't a dream, then? Right, here goes," and as he thought it the cup of tea appeared.

"Whoa, this is something else. Coffee for me, please, and toast. Can I get you another cup, May, or some more toast maybe?"

"More coffee would be nice thank you, George." With that it appeared in front of them.

George, acting as if it was second nature by now, took Iris's tea in to her and then rejoined May at the kitchen table.

Tucking into his coffee and toast, he said, "I think we'll have to take things more slowly with Iris. She isn't quite as adaptable as me."

"I agree but I think you could be surprised how easily she has accepted all that has happened, Shasta affects people in many different ways, George, and you could find that Iris changes her view completely during her stay. I assume you will be staying until Shasta returns?"

"Oh definitely, we must" he said.

"We must what?" asked Iris as she came into the kitchen holding her empty cup and saucer.

"Stay here until Shasta returns."

"Well that goes without question, my dear."

How easily they accept the change from Summer to Shasta,

thought May.

"Would you like another cup of tea, Iris?" asked May with a hint of devilment.

"Oh, yes please, that would be lovely, May."

Instantly Iris's cup was full and she was so shocked she nearly dropped it. "How did you do that? I mean, it happened instantly. May, how..."

George just smiled and beckoned Iris to sit on his knee. Surprised at herself, she actually did it. How many years was it since she had sat on his knee, she wondered. At least six, she supposed. Well what was happening to her? She had to admit whatever it was she liked it very much.

Staying where she was she began to drink her tea. I really fancy some toast, May, if that's alright."

May and George looked at one another and smiled secretively. The look on Iris' face should have been captured in print when the toast appeared. She was in shock at first and just looked at it incredulously. Then hunger got the better of her and she began to eat it, making no comment whatsoever.

Whilst May was clearing the breakfast crockery, George and Iris returned to the bedroom to tidy up and make the bed, and George took the opportunity to discuss with Iris what had happened to their daughter. Given the circumstances, Iris took it all very well and in her stride. They should in all honesty be worried sick but somehow they both felt that everything would work out alright.

Having made the bed between them, Iris glided over to George and put her arms around him. *Well, this is different*, thought George. *I have never known Iris to be so demonstrative. May was right - this village does have a different effect on people*, and this for Iris was very different. 'One doesn't usually bother with that sort of thing', was her usual comment.

Eventually they left the bedroom and went back out to May in the kitchen.

"Perhaps we could all go for a walk to the village as it's such a beautiful day," said May.

"I rather like that idea. What do you think, Iris?"

"Whatever you say, George dear," said Iris rather shyly.

May was very aware of the difference in her sister. She seemed less anxious than when she first came. It certainly made life easier for her and also for George.

Poor George, in marrying Iris he had taken on a lifetime's work. She could be so pompous at times but he loved her dearly and gave into her most of the time. Every so often, though, he put up a defiant streak which brought Iris back into line.

"Well, if we're ready, lets go," said May.

Walking up the path to the gate, May stopped every so often to admire her flowers and praise them for their beauty. Iris and George, following behind, did the same.

"I was just thinking, George, perhaps we should change the design of our garden when we get back home. I do believe our garden is far too stiff and regimented."

"Did I just hear you right? When I suggested we have it rustic and rambling you stopped talking to me for a day merely because I had suggested it. It's taken Giles, our gardener, at least ten years to get it exactly as you wanted it and now you want it all gutted and started again. Well, rather you tell him than me, Iris."

"Don't be such a fuddy-duddy, George, I'll talk to Giles when I get back. You know I have a way with him."

May laughed quietly to herself. Oh yes things were going to be perfect and she might even take Iris and George to Faery Cove sooner rather than later. She couldn't wait to see her sister's face, or George's for that matter. Having to be reduced in size was going to be quite an experience for both of them.

During their walk to the village, Iris and George commented on the many styles of garden there were in Shasta without a weed to be seen.

"They must spend an exceptional amount of time caring for their gardens, May," said Iris.

Was this the opportunity to remind Iris about Shasta being a magic village, she wondered. Perhaps not; she would wait until they stopped for a drink in the village.

"Oh, I don't think they have too much to do, Iris. The gardens more or less look after themselves," said May grinning.

Chapter 22

Having reached the village, May suggested that they should have a drink to cool themselves.

Close to the village green was a teashop, typical of the type found in Devon with quaint tables and chairs arranged outside. Iris chose a table under a tree where she could look over the village green and enjoy the shade. George sat in the chair beside her, on May's insistence, while she went inside to get their drinks. Iris had been persuaded to have a fresh cold orange juice along with George and May.

"I can't believe how incredibly relaxed I feel here, George. I know I should be worried sick about Shasta but I trust May."

Hearing this last remark as she came out with the tray, May smiled to herself. "Well I'm pleased to hear that, Iris."

Setting the tray down, she put a glass of juice in front of George and Iris, sat down in the spare seat, and settled back contentedly to watch the world go by.

Iris was sipping her drink and looking out over the green when suddenly a startled look came over her face. George noticed it asked, "Are you alright, Iris?"

"Well, I'm not sure to be honest, George. As I looked at the green I thought I saw a maypole and Morris dancers which reminded me of an old-fashioned village fair. It's probably just my imagination running wild and the heat, I suppose. I'm not used to it."

May felt now was the time to take a chance and tell Iris the truth about Shasta Village.

"Actually, Iris, it's quite possible that you did see what you thought. Every year for the past two hundred years or more there has been a fair on the village green. The villagers take the opportunity to dress up in costumes of old and re-enact their past history. The fair normally lasts for one day only but when your

106

daughter, Shasta, arrived in the village recently, she declared that we would celebrate for two days this time."

"I know I said earlier that I trusted you, May, because you are my sister, but I find it rather hard to come to terms with the fact that my daughter is Shasta, and that she is here in the village but living in the past at the moment."

Feeling desperately sorry for her sister, May said, "Try and understand, Iris, that Shasta is a magical village. You remarked yourself about the gardens. The villagers only have to wish for what they want in their gardens and it grows instantly. When Shasta came here two hundred years ago, it was a weed-infested village that no one cared about. By casting a spell with the help of the villagers, she ensured that from that moment on never again would a weed grow in Shasta, and so it has been ever since. If you want something to happen in Shasta, it happens."

"Are you telling me that I just had a glimpse of the past, May?"

"Well, actually, Iris, yes, I believe you did. I was unsure at first whether you had inherited the gift, but it would seem you have."

"What gift, May? What is she talking about, George?"

George, who had been sitting quietly listening to all of this, suddenly became more interested and sat forward in his chair. "What exactly do you mean, May?" he asked.

"The females in the family have the gift of second sight. You have not been aware of it, Iris, because until now it hasn't materialised. However, because you're in Shasta, it has been awoken. That is why you had a glimpse of the past."

Iris was sitting quietly trying to take all this in.

"Is that why I feel so different in Shasta, May? So much more relaxed?"

"Yes," said May. "The longer you stay, the more acceptable it will become to you."

May went back inside the teashop to refill their glasses, giving Iris a chance to take it all in. Magic wasn't always used outside of their own homes.

"Are you alright, Iris?" asked George with concern. "That's rather a lot to take in all at once."

"Well, it is a bit of a shock, but I have always had this feeling about our family. The way May comes across, for instance, with her long black plaited hair virtually down to her waist. That in itself is unusual for a woman of her age these days, and all those gold and silver bangles and long flowing dresses that she wears. Sometimes I'm sure there is a Romany influence. Actually I feel quite excited about it George if I'm honest," she said.

"You never cease to amaze me, Iris" said George in a loving way.

May came back with their refilled glasses and they sat back in a companionable silence enjoying the cooling drink, taking in the ambience of village life in general.

As May looked out towards the village green, she was suddenly aware that someone was approaching from behind them. Resisting the urge to turn around, she knew instinctively that it was Erasmus.

"Hello, May. How are you today?" he asked.

"I'm very well, thank you, Erasmus. Can I introduce you to my sister, Iris, and her husband, George?"

When the introductions had been made, Erasmus was invited to join them for a drink but this he declined, not wanting to intrude. Having bid them farewell, he made his way across the green, telling May that he would see her later on.

"What a good looking man Erasmus is, May. How did you meet him?" Iris asked, full of curiosity.

May being a private person was reluctant to talk about Erasmus but her sister would not let it go until she had heard the whole story.

"Very well, Iris, I met Erasmus on Shasta Day quite by accident. We got talking and he gave me a love token for my hair and we have been walking out ever since."

"Well, I must admit you're a quiet one, May. I had no idea. Can you explain about the love token, though. I really don't

108

understand?"

"Well, as I said we met on Shasta Day. On this day, the whole village dresses up in historical costume as the mood takes them. Everyone congregates on the village green and all of the old traditions are performed as in days of yore. Sometimes we even revert to using the old dialect. If a man is interested in a woman, he will give her a ribbon to wear in her hair. I suppose it could be compared to the commitment of an engagement ring. If she accepts and wears it, a love tryst is then assumed and the couple will then go out together until such times as they marry. Erasmus gave me a ribbon and I have worn it ever since. It was all rather sudden, I must admit. I don't know if it's love at first sight, but it feels right."

"Oh, May, how romantic," said Iris. "I must admit I never thought you would be the marrying kind. I am so pleased for you. Isn't it wonderful, George?"

George agreed. He was very fond of May and only too pleased to see her happy. He was not unaware of the gentle flush on her cheeks, as Erasmus had spoken to her. He considered her an attractive woman and would like to see her settle down with someone but there was something about Erasmus he wasn't too sure about. Perhaps he was being over-protective of May and only time would tell.

Chapter 23

The past

It had been a beautiful hot summer's day and the young woman sat atop her brightly coloured caravan enjoying the last rays of the early evening sunshine and the beginning of a welcome light breeze. The reins of her piebald horse were lying loosely across her foot beneath her dress and he seemed to reflect her happiness as he trotted slowly along the country lane. The sun, still very warm, was gradually sinking in the sky behind the trees but, every so often, it appeared through the thin branches.

Listening to the birds singing in the trees, the woman was at one with the elements.

The hedgerows along the lane also gave cover to the birds which talked to her as she passed by.

"Good morning, mistress," they seemed to be saying.

"Good morning to you, pied wagtails and sparrows," she responded in kind.

Approaching a fork in the road, she instinctively encouraged the horse to the right. Suddenly she reined the horse in and decided on impulse to go left. As the young woman slowly made her way along the leafy lane, she was aware that she was approaching a village. It looked completely neglected and, from every grass verge and garden, weeds ran rampantly.

How awful that there should be such neglect, she reflected. No flowers were growing at all.

As she passed the villagers, their heads were hung low as if in despair.

"Good evening, sir," she called to one, but the only response was a low grunt of derision.

As she reached the middle of the village, she reined in her horse and got into the back of the wagon. Picking up her black cooking pot, she set it down outside, balancing it on its three legs, and placed some dried seed pods and fresh herbs inside it. Collecting a few twigs from nearby she placed them under the pot and proceeded to light a fire underneath it.

Out of curiosity, the local villagers began to gather round.

The look of the woman was strange to them. She had blonde hair worn in a long plait over one shoulder, compared to the villagers' hair which was mostly shades of brown or black.

The villagers grew in confidence as their number began to increase.

Picking a stick up from the ground, the woman began to stir the contents of the pot from which a strange but hypnotic pungent smell began to rise.

The villagers, sitting around in a semicircle with their smocks coming over the knees of their britches, seemed to be affected by the aroma and they started to smile. Nodding their heads in approval, they were happy to sit there watching. The woman began to hum quietly to herself whilst stirring the contents. One by one the villagers joined in the humming and took it in turns to stir the pot, nodding happily towards the woman.

As the vigil progressed through the night, the sky began to lighten into a new dawn and the woman held up her hand to command attention.

"My friends, each of you will take one seed pod from the pot. When you open it, you will see two seeds. Plant one of the seeds in the hedgerow and the second seed in each of your gardens. Every one will be different and this should be done at sunset tonight."

As they had nothing to lose, the villagers put their trust in the woman and did as she asked. The following morning, in each garden and every hedgerow, a new flower had grown where each weed had been. The villagers were so happy to see so many pretty flowers, they asked the woman if they could name the village after her.

Smiling, she agreed and the village became known as Shasta after her.

Many white Shasta daisies now grew in profusion alongside the red poppies in the hedgerows. In celebration, they decided to hold a fayre on the village green and Shasta was asked to stay and join them. It would be held two days hence, on the Saturday, as many preparations had to be made.

One woman from the village called May, who appeared to be in her late thirties, asked Shasta to join her in a meal that evening.

"I should be very happy to join you, May, and I thank you," she said.

Shasta asked May to sit in the front of the wagon with her and they slowly made their way up from the village green to the cottage.

Words were not considered necessary as they were content in each other's company.

Approaching the door of the cottage, May lifted the haggaday, or door latch, to gain entry.

As Shasta followed May inside she became very aware of the spaciousness of the room compared to her wagon. Glancing around, Shasta tried to take everything in at once.

Although there was only one well-proportioned room, she was instantly drawn towards the large fireplace. On either side was a wooden chair.

On the right hand side of the fire hearth was a black pittering iron for stoking the fire. This was leaning against a box of logs filled to the brim. On the other side of the hearth, resting on its back, was a smoothing iron ready for use.

Hanging from a hook concealed somewhere in the chimney breast was a black cooking pot suspended over the lit fire.

Shasta inhaled the wondrous smell of meat, herbs and vegetables invading the room which made her realise just how hungry she was. She was later to learn it was not uncommon for a cooking pot such as this to be kept permanently topped up over a lit fire so that there was always food ready to eat.

Shasta only cooked her food when she made a stop on the road, usually by a stream.

On a black trivet, a revel cake was cooling, a favourite of Shasta's which she had made herself many times in the past. The ingredients of dark flour, currants and caraway seeds were purchased from the villages as she passed through them.

To the back of the room was a table with a few unmatched chairs spaced around it. On the other side, in the corner, appeared to be the sleeping quarters which contained two wooden pallets with mattresses on top. A long curtain hung in between, separating them.

This left Shasta wondering who the other occupant might be.

As she was preoccupied with this thought, the door to the cottage burst open and a young man entered.

Dressed in normal working clothes of a smock down to his knees and breeches, he appeared to be about twenty years old. He walked over towards May and, lifting her off her feet, he proceeded to dance with her around the room, much to both of their amusement.

Shasta was instantly taken by his good looks. Aware that she was staring she cast her eyes downwards.

Setting May back on her feet he said, "Hello, May. I heard in the village that we had a guest staying."

"Shasta, this is Merlin. He has lived with me since he was a young lad and I'm convinced he has never grown up."

As Shasta looked properly into the young man's eyes, she was completely overwhelmed by her feelings. Very shyly, she bobbed down in a curtsey. Normally unaffected by young men she had met in the past, Merlin made her feel quite warm inside from her toes to the top of her head. She was also aware that her face felt rather hot.

Merlin gave a quick bob of his head to Shasta whilst at the same time taking in her beauty.

"I'm very pleased to meet you, mistress Shasta," he said.

May, noticing the looks that passed between the young couple, was pleased. Merlin had never shown any interest in the local girls of the village and, although she had only just met Shasta, she was already becoming quite fond of her.

"I suggest you go outside and clean up, Merlin, then we can eat. I assume you will be coming back down to the village with us tonight to help with the preparations for the festivities," she said.

"Very well, May, and, yes, I will come with you. I'm looking forward to it."

"Will you get the dishes from the shelf please, Shasta, and I will dish up our meal," May asked.

"Of course," she said.

Reaching to the shelf, Shasta put the dishes on the table, still preoccupied with thoughts of Merlin.

May took the dishes one by one and filled them with meat, potatoes and a selection of root vegetables. As she filled the last dish, Merlin re-entered the cottage and took his place at the table.

Over their meal, Shasta explained that she hadn't really intended to come to this village but had intended to go in the opposite direction. She couldn't explain why she had been drawn towards it.

"That was absolutely wonderful, May. I didn't realise how hungry I was. Thank you," said Shasta, having finished her meal.

Merlin agreed. Standing up he walked over to the revel cake and brought it back to the table with a knife.

Cutting three pieces, he cut a further four thin pieces which were put aside for good luck, as was the custom.

Offering a piece to Shasta as their guest, he gave a piece to May and finally himself.

When this was eaten, May and Shasta each had a mug of ginger beer while Merlin had a mug of ale, and they sat back replete.

Having rested awhile, they made their way slowly down to the village to soak up the atmosphere.

Many of the villagers who passed Shasta looked on her with

reverence. The men tugged their forelocks whilst the women bobbed a curtsey in respect. At the same time they thanked her again for making their village so pleasing to the eye.

Shasta had never felt happier. As long as she could remember, she had always been a traveller. Now, for the first time, her wanderlust didn't have the same appeal and she felt that she could possibly settle here in the village so recently called after her.

Chapter 24

As they reached the green, Shasta could hear lots of laughter in the distance.

Her thoughts travelled back to the despondency in the villagers when she had arrived. Fortune certainly had smiled on her when she had taken the left fork in the road.

She would never have met May or Merlin otherwise.

"You seem happy, mistress," said May.

"I was just remembering how it was when I arrived in the village, May. Everyone seemed so unhappy and disillusioned. Now everyone has a smile on their face."

"They have good reason to be happy, Shasta," said Merlin. "The village has been transformed and we have the added pleasure of a beautiful young woman in our midst."

"Thank you, kind sir," she said with an exaggerated curtsey while in kind Merlin bowed to her.

May looked on with contentment at the young couple and began to daydream. *Who knows*, she thought, *maybe if we could persuade Shasta to stay Merlin could find the happiness he deserves.*

Approaching the village green in the warmth of the summer evening, Shasta looked on with wonderment.

In the centre of the green a huge bonfire was being prepared. In the distance, large spits were already in place to roast the bulls which would certainly feed the whole community.

Shasta took it on herself to suggest that a tree be cut down from the forest on the day before the fayre. She had seen this done during her travels. A female entering puberty then performed a sacred ritual for the purification of the earth. Shasta was asked if she would choose the tree and oversee the ritual, to which she agreed. The thought of a fayre and celebration caused great excitement among the villagers and they looked forward to it with excited anticipation. As dusk began to fall, Shasta, May and Merlin walked back to the cottage. Shasta retired to her caravan having bid May and Merlin a good night.

She began to think about the events of the last couple of days and her feelings for Merlin. She had met many young men on her travels but none had affected her in the way that Merlin had. With that in her mind, she decided to go to bed and finally fell asleep after much restlessness.

She awoke at the crack of dawn and, preparing herself a substantial breakfast, she made her way down the path towards May's cottage. May had insisted that she leave the caravan on the grass verge in front of the cottage.

At the cottage door May and Merlin stood waiting for her.

"Good morning, mistress Shasta," they said in unison.

"Good morning to you both," she responded.

"Tis a beautiful morning, mistress" said Merlin using his natural dialect.

"Aye, it be," she responded in kind. "The forest will be beautiful at this time of the morning," and she quickened her steps in anticipation.

As they approached the forest the villagers had already begun to gather.

"Morning, mistress," they called in reverence as she passed them by.

As she acknowledged each one in turn, they were happy to let her take control of events.

Selecting a tree to be cut down, Shasta was aware of a young girl hovering uncertainly close by. Calling her over, Shasta asked her name.

"If you please, mistress, I am given the name Beth," she said bobbing in a curtsey.

"Well, let's walk into the forest together while the tree is being cut down."

117

Beth walked beside Shasta with some trepidation, unsure of what was expected of her. Shasta sensed her discomfort, and explained that they would be collecting some mulched earth from beneath the pine trees and various herbs that grew wild from deep within the forest. These would be mixed together in a certain fashion. Still deep within the forest, with Shasta's guidance, Beth would silently perform the ceremony for the purification of the earth. This was not for the other villagers' eyes and Shasta swore Beth to secrecy. The following year she would be expected to show the next young maiden what to do, and so it would be passed on.

Returning with Beth to the outskirts of the forest, Shasta was pleased to see that the tree had already been felled. Leaving Beth, she walked towards it. The fresh smell of the pine overpowered her and, kneeling down, she held her face within the branches purely for the pleasure of being at one with nature. The villagers stood slightly back from her in awe, unsure what to do. As she stood up and turned to the villagers, she somehow looked more imposing.

Lifting her arms up, Shasta spoke. "People of Shasta, Beth has performed the sacred ritual. It will remain her secret until one year hence when she alone will reveal it to the next maiden. The month of August occurs at Litha time, a period of summer governed by the moon. When I first arrived in Shasta every garden and hedgerow was infested with weeds. By working together and planting seeds cultivated during the moonlight, we have changed the village to what it is today. From this day forth, this tree cutting ceremony will be known as 'Weodmonath', or weed month. It will be performed ever year on this day as a reminder to us of what the village was originally like. Flowers will grow at will in permanent sunshine. At night a gentle rain will fall to allow the flowers and crops to drink their fill. Whatever you wish to grow in Shasta will flourish. Let all the villagers return to the green and we will erect the tree ready for the festivities. So let it be."

Whilst six of the strongest men stayed behind to carry the tree down to the village, Shasta, Merlin and May followed the villagers.

Although they had welcomed Shasta into their home, May and Merlin were also a bit awe-struck by the change in Shasta, and walked beside her with renewed respect.

Shasta sensed this and instantly put them at their ease. Speaking to them both, she reminded them that they had taken her into their home, fed her and made her feel welcome. For that she would always be grateful.

May thought about this on their walk to the village and at the earliest opportunity asked Merlin if perhaps Shasta could share their home with them. Merlin thought this was a wonderful idea as it would give him the opportunity to get to know Shasta better.

Shasta, having the gift of second sight since birth, knew their thoughts but decided to wait to be asked whenever May was ready.

Eventually May approached Shasta with the subject, unsure if their home would be suitable for her. She need not have been concerned as Shasta instantly agreed to the idea. The caravan would remain on the grass verge by the cottage, though, in case she ever felt the urge to wander or just to sleep in her familiar surroundings. The locals would tend to the horse and Shasta could visit him often.

On reaching the village green, Shasta noticed that the villagers had formed two lines, with the men and women facing one another. May and Merlin tagged onto the end of the line while Shasta moved to the front in readiness for the tree to arrive.

The anticipation and excitement filtered through the crowd as the arrival of the tree had now become a major part of the festivities.

As the men came into view carrying the tree, a silence came over the crowd. Beth, who walked very solemnly, conscious of the important part she had played in the ritual, preceded it. Slowly, it made its way through the line towards Shasta while each villager in turn touched the branches with reverence. On reaching Shasta, they stopped and waited uncertain of what to do next. Shasta felt an

119

uncontrollable urge once more to bury her face in the branches of the tree and, in doing so, was entwined with Mother Nature herself.

As she drew her head up, she instructed that the tree be stripped of its' branches and that these should then be placed over the doors of each house along with flowers of choice.

The local carpenter should carve a wooden crown in the shape designated by her and it should then be painted gold. Around the crown would be more flowers and the maidens would tie long lengths of coloured ribbon from it which would touch the ground. Caught up with enthusiasm, the villagers started to strip the branches, each taking their requirements to decorate their houses. Meanwhile the carpenter hurried away to find the finest piece of yew with which to make the crown. Perfection, to his mind, would take a good few hours, even with his skills. The maidens in their excitement scurried back and forth. Each had the task of finding at least one piece of ribbon to suit the requirements and to prepare their finest costumes to wear.

Shasta looked on with contentment. *How wonderful*, she thought again, *to see such a change in the villagers*. This fayre tomorrow would surely be a day to remember and talked about during the perpetual sunny days of the future.

Shasta the village would surely have a magical future.

Chapter 25

From the crack of dawn the villagers were up and about. This was not unusual, except this morning there was an air of excitement everywhere.

All the tasks set by Shasta had been adhered to, to the letter, each villager helping his neighbours to decorate their houses. Maidens dashed in and out of friends' houses, trying on clothes and swapping them with each other to ensure that everyone felt their best, most hoping that the young men would make love trysts with the giving of ribbons. The air of expectancy was electric.

Children in small groups collected spring flowers. Making little posies, they went from door to door chanting a rhyme

Flowers, flowers, high-do
Sheeny, greeny, rino
Sheeny, greeny, sheeney Greeny,
Rum, tum, fra

Normally this would only be done on Shrove Tuesday and they would be given a morsel to eat. However, as everyone was entering into the spirit of the atmosphere, they were mostly given the odd coin to spend at the fayre.

By working late into the night, the carpenter had made and painted the gold crown to sit on top of the tree. Two strong lads had balanced a third lad on their shoulders with the task of placing the crown on the now upright and secured tree. This was much to the amusement and admiration of the young girls watching. The ribbons would later be attached in the same way.

By late morning the green began to fill with people. The two spits had a bull on each being slowly roasted to be ready by early evening. Young women wandered about in their finery with flowers in their hair in the hope of being noticed by the men. Older women had also made a special effort but more in the spirit of fun than the hope of finding a lover.

In the distance men were getting ready to take part in various games of running, archery and casting stones whilst, out of harm's way, others were preparing to chance their arm at throwing javelins. Young boys, in a bid to impress the girls, were taking part in sack races. Then, balancing on a greasy pole with their legs gripped underneath, it was their main objective to knock their opponents off with cushions or pillows.

Vendors called out telling of their wares of love hearts and ribbons which were bought by lovers. The men then entwined the ribbons in their loved one's hair.

Six Morris dancers dressed in white, bedecked with ribbons and flowers on their black hats and bells on their shoes, awaited the arrival of Shasta when they would begin their intricate dance with the ribbons already hanging from the tree. At the completion of the dance, the ribbons would form a plait from top to bottom as dictated by the old custom. Once this was done they would also perform a dance with wooden staves which were hit together in the air and on the ground in a strict order.

Children were running around chasing a squealing pig more for amusement than out of any expectation of catching it. Occasionally it tripped up some folk by darting in and out of the legs of groups of villagers. One rather rotund gentleman wearing a large black flat hat took a step backward, overbalanced and fell over the pig, much to the amusement of all around him. Getting back on his feet with difficulty and replacing his hat, he carried on his conversation with an amused smile on his face as if nothing was amiss.

Some of the women wore frocks with white aprons on top, whilst others favoured frocks with a shawl. On their heads they had white mobcaps or straw hats with sprays of flowers cut from their gardens. Others favoured wearing the flowers in their hair which was a new experience in itself. The men mostly wore white smocks with stitching at the chest, breeches tied at the knees or ankles, and black round hats with brims.

At midday Shasta arrived with May and Merlin. Instantly a hush fell everywhere. Sensing that something important was expected of her, Shasta became rather embarrassed. This situation still felt new to her. Seeing the Morris dancers standing by the tree expectantly, she sensed that she should begin the proceedings.

"People of Shasta," she began, "by weaving all of the ribbons on this tree together as one, the people of the village will also be forever as one. Our thoughts will always be harmonious and we will ensure that our neighbours are never wanting. So let it be."

As Shasta finished speaking, a very strange feeling came over her and her head began to throb and spin. She staggered slightly as images began to swim in front of her eyes. She had a strong sense that this had all happened before.

Merlin was instantly by her side while May hovered nearby.

"Are you not well, mistress?" he asked with concern.

"Thank you for your concern, Merlin. I am well, so let us begin." This was said much more sharply than she had intended.

Instantly the music began. The Morris dancers had taken up their positions, each holding a ribbon ready to begin the dance. The villagers clapped in time to the music whilst one young lad dived into the middle of the dancers and tried to confuse them, much to their annoyance. He was instantly and unceremoniously removed by a harassed parent.

At the completion of the dance the villagers broke out into spontaneous applause and cheering before breaking up into little groups of their choosing to begin taking part in the festivities.

May and Merlin moved away from Shasta, sensing that she needed to be alone.

As she walked, Shasta tried to come to terms with the myriad of thoughts passing through her mind.

She needed to be alone for a while to put her clairvoyant skills into action. Normally it was instantaneous but her mind was confused. Slowly, head bent and deep in thought, she made her way to the edge of the green. The villagers made space for her to pass through their groups.

Reaching the edge of the green, Shasta sat for a while on the grass. She clasped her arms round her bent knees and, with eyes closed, lifted her face to the sun. It warmed her and gave clarity to her thoughts.

As the sun's rays danced in front of her closed eyes, she imagined she saw a rainbow of colours almost like small prisms. Unexplainable thoughts of faeries and wishing wells began to infiltrate her thoughts, and the name Abelia came into her mind. With a jolt her eyes flew open. She knew that name, but from where? Rubbing her temples with her index fingers, she tried to focus her mind. It was as if her powers had been removed temporarily. Why couldn't she make the connection? It was all there; only the key was missing.

Getting to her feet Shasta was aware that there were very few people at this end of the green.

May was nowhere to be seen, but Merlin was sitting on the grass a short distance away watching her closely with a concerned look on his face. As their eyes met, his face broke into a smile and he stood and walked towards her.

As he reached her, he automatically held both his hands out to her and she, in need of comfort, took them. For a moment she seemed to melt against him but she regained her composure, removed her hands and looked into his face.

"Are you alright, mistress? You seem very troubled," he asked.

"I'm not sure, Merlin. My thoughts are very confused at the moment."

Merlin held out his hand to her. At first she was hesitant but natural instinct took over and she graciously accepted his offer as they wandered around and soaked up the atmosphere.

Nevertheless, Shasta had to work hard to shrug off her growing sense of concern.

Chapter 26

The present

May was relaxing in the garden swing seat enjoying the late afternoon sun.

This was her favourite place and the swing had been deliberately placed so that she could enjoy the last rays of the sun each day as it set behind the trees near Faery Cove.

It also gave her an opportunity to drink in the heady perfume from the jasmine, honeysuckle, sweet peas and lavender growing close by. In the distance sunflowers, hollyhocks and foxgloves stood smartly to attention. Forget-me-nots and lily of the valley peeped out shyly at ground level.

George and Iris were lying a little way off on the grass, partially hidden by the fruit trees, enjoying their own company.

George was gently snoozing in the sun with a hat over his face, whilst Iris was absorbed in a *Country Garden* magazine.

Since her sister had arrived in Shasta, May could not believe the difference that had taken place in her.

Iris had changed virtually overnight.

Initially she had been very highly strung and on edge, but now she was completely relaxed and accepting all that Shasta had to offer her.

This had made things a lot easier for May. She had been reluctant to tell her about the village and its magical qualities. Perhaps tonight she would visit Faery Cove when her sister was in bed and talk to Abelia the faery queen about bringing them for a visit.

By sunset they had eaten and May suggested a slow walk to the village. She secretly hoped that maybe she would also see Erasmus. He had stayed away while her family had been visiting, even though he had been invited to eat with them on several occasions.

Both George and Iris agreed that a walk would be enjoyable and they slowly made their way toward the village green.

Iris took a great interest in the gardens as she passed each one, gathering ideas for the complete transformation of her own garden. She hadn't made up her mind yet as to how she would approach their gardener. He had spent many years cultivating her flowers and lawns to perfection, and now she intended to completely change it and turn it into a cottage garden with flowers growing where the mood took them.

George had been astonished and insisted that she be the one to approach their gardener. Although he had heard him muttering many times about how 'Her Ladyship' wanted this and that, perhaps it would suit him better and be less work in the long run. However that was for Iris to deal with, not him.

Strange that he hadn't given his own garden centre in Holland another thought since he had been in Shasta. Henney, his manager, would contact him if there were any news.

On reaching the village they decided to stop for a drink by the green. Already sitting at one of the tables enjoying a cool drink was Erasmus. Seeing May approach, he stood to welcome her. His face lit up and he smiled at her full of happiness. May, catching sight of him, increased her pace.

Erasmus took hold of her hands and kissed May full on the mouth, taking her by surprise. In turn her face reflected her joy in seeing him.

George and Iris, in the meantime, had taken themselves inside the tearoom to get their drinks, giving May a few minutes alone with Erasmus.

"Oh, Erasmus, I have missed you. How are you?" she asked.

"I have missed you too, May. Can we meet soon?"

May pondered on this for a few moments, then, seeing George and Iris returning with the drinks, she said quietly, "Come to the cottage at midnight. I will be in the garden. We can talk then."

The four of them sat talking for an hour or so, while they enjoyed their drinks and the atmosphere of village life.

Erasmus amused George and Iris with his anecdotes about the village while May contributed her own stories from time to time.

George then explained about the problems with his garden centre in Holland. Erasmus sympathised with him but, rising from his seat, said he had to leave. Bending to kiss May, he bade them all farewell and made his way back to the other side of the village.

Iris, being completely won over by him, suggested that May had been as lucky in love as she herself was with George. With that she spontaneously took George's hand, much to his delight.

As the three of them walked slowly back to the cottage, Iris and May were in deep conversation. This gave George an opportunity to think about Erasmus and mull his initial feelings of uncertainty about him.

He had to admit he had enjoyed his company tonight, and his feelings for May were very obvious by the sidelong glances that he had given her at every opportunity. Perhaps his thoughts were unfounded after all and he was being over-protective towards May as usual. He loved his wife dearly but, if truth were known, maybe he was just a little bit jealous of Erasmus.

By the time they reached the cottage it was nearly ten o'clock. Iris declared that the walk had made her thirsty and suggested that they have a final drink in the cool of the garden before they went to bed.

Iris sat in the swing seat whilst George and May sat at the table. Eager to try out some magic, Iris asked what they wanted and she would produce it.

"Don't forget that it will appear as soon as we tell you," said May.

"Why don't you choose for us?" suggested George.

"Alright, let's have three beers, then," she said.

The child within her laughed happily when they appeared in front of them.

George, surprised by her choice, began to drink his straightaway whilst watching Iris gradually work her way through hers, much to his amusement. He still couldn't get over the change in his wife. After several years of her being so straight-laced, this was a refreshing change. He hoped that she would maintain this new image long after they left Shasta.

May was sitting in her favourite seat enjoying her own company. The moon was shining brightly and a light rain was falling, enabling everything in the garden to drink greedily. Her brother-in-law and sister were now in bed, and she could spend this time thinking about Erasmus while she waited for him to arrive. She loved him dearly but her feelings would have to be postponed until Shasta and Merlin returned. She missed them dreadfully and constantly wondered what was happening. Shasta insisted that this was something she and Merlin must do alone and she had to respect that. So, without preamble, she had put all her 'gifts' on hold concerning the couple. She wasn't one to tempt fate in any way. It was strange to think that they were in this village but two hundred years in the past.

Her place for the moment was here supporting her sister Iris and George.

"Hello, May."

Erasmus had come quietly into the garden and had been watching her secretively for some time, almost reluctant to interrupt her thoughts.

"Erasmus! You startled me. I didn't hear you arrive. Come and sit beside me."

Settling himself, he laid his arm across the back of the seat.

"What were you thinking so deeply about, May?" he asked.

"I was just wondering about Shasta and Merlin."

Although May and Erasmus had taken many moonlight walks in her garden, she had never taken him as far as the wishing well and gate which were the entrance to Faery Cove. This was mainly because she sensed that he hadn't been quite ready to meet Abelia.

"Since Shasta left with Merlin my power of clairvoyance is not as strong as usual. Maybe it's because I'm so concerned for them," she offered as an excuse.

"If you feel it would help, I will be happy to come with you to Faery Cove, and there is no time like the present."

May was surprised but happy with this gesture. She hadn't expected him to offer so readily.

Slowly they walked to the wishing well at the bottom of the garden.

On the way, she explained that they had to drink from the water in the well in order to make them smaller in size. Erasmus thought this was rather amusing, but excitement tinged with apprehension began to creep in. She also explained that they would meet several faeries that would guide them to Abelia.

On reaching the well, May dipped the cup into the water and scooped up enough for them both to drink. Instantly the trees surrounding the garden began to tower over them. Instinctively she took hold of Erasmus' hand. The look on his face was indescribable and it made her giggle.

"Are you alright, Erasmus?" she asked.

"Well, I must admit I wasn't really sure what to expect, but being this small I hope we don't meet any animals bigger than us."

"Don't worry. We'll be safe, I promise you," May said.

Not quite convinced, Erasmus began to glance around him. Women naturally expected a man to protect them, but this was literally a new world to him and he was preparing to expect the unexpected.

As he turned round, he noticed a small circle of lights in the distance quite close to the ground.

"What's that, May?" he asked with some trepidation, hoping that she would have the answer.

"They are the faeries come to escort us to Abelia. After all, she is the Queen of the Faeries."

May noticed that the faeries were standing off in the distance, seemingly reluctant to approach. As a regular visitor they recognised May instantly, but they were obviously unsure of Erasmus.

May suggested that he stayed back a few paces to give her the opportunity to explain his presence. Moving forward towards the circle of light, May explained that he was a friend and that they need not be frightened.

While May was talking to them, Erasmus took in the details of their dresses. Everyone who believed in faeries had their own idea of what they looked like and he was no different. Just because he was a man, it didn't mean that he couldn't believe in them, even if he didn't advertise it. Actually he thought they looked just as he had imagined them, but far more exquisite.

Most of them were wearing beautiful gossamer dresses that looked as if it had been spun by spiders.

The faery approaching him was wearing a beautiful yellow dress which reminded him of a pale sun. Her hair was blonde and curly and, woven in and out of the curls, was jasmine blossom and ivy. In her hand she held a stem of jasmine. She hesitated slightly and shyly introduced herself.

"My name is Princess Jasmine," she said importantly.

"I'm very pleased to meet you," said Erasmus with some amusement and feeling less nervous than before.

This had given the other faeries courage and a second approached him wearing an identical dress but it was bright orange. On top of her blonde hair was the bloom of a day lily. Much like Jasmine, this faery held a white flowering lily.

"My name is Princess Day Lily," she said equally importantly.

"I'm very pleased to meet you also," said Erasmus.

One by one they came to introduce themselves. He noted that they were all similarly dressed. Interwoven in their hair were various flowers depending on which flower they represented. Apart from the two princesses, each of the faeries carried paper lanterns lit by glow-worms. As each faery moved, a faint rainbow coloured dust seemed to fall about them.

"Now it's my turn," said a voice.

It seemed to come from even closer to the ground. Erasmus had been almost at eye level with most of the faeries but he had to bend even lower to see this one.

"What is your name?" asked Erasmus

"My name is Evening Primrose and I am second in command after Queen Abelia."

Dressed in a brighter yellow than Princess Jasmine, she had the bloom of an evening primrose perched jauntily on the side of her head. In her hand she carried a stem of evening primrose which seemed to glow much lighter in the moonlight.

Turning sharply she sent a cloud of faery dust into the air. "Come," she said. "We must not keep the Queen waiting. She has been expecting you, May."

"How did the Queen know that you were coming, May?" enquired Erasmus.

"Abelia knows everything. Her powers are far superior to mine, my dear," she said.

With that, she started to follow the group of faeries who held their lanterns aloft to enable them to see where they were going.

Singing as they walked along, their voices sounded just like wind chimes tinkling in the breeze.

Looking around him as they walked, Erasmus noted that forget-me-nots and blue bells grew in profusion around the base of tree trunks. Meandering in and out at will grew Hedra ivy, which clung to the trunk of trees. It was difficult to accept that this was all still part of May's garden.

"Halt."

The command, spoken quietly but sharply by Evening Primrose, brought Erasmus out of his thoughts. May beside him came to a standstill.

"Ah, May, welcome to our kingdom once again. Your friend Erasmus finally decided to visit us, then?"

Abelia was sitting on a small throne shaped from a lavender bush, dressed in what looked like pure silver which seemed to shimmer in the moonlight. Unlike the dresses of the other faeries, this dress touched the ground. On her feet were silver and gold slippers which curled up slightly at the end. To complete her ensemble, a small crown of silver and gold, encrusted with tiny hanging crystals which sparkled in the moonlight, sat firmly on her head.

Behind the throne, standing on either side of her, were the two princesses, Jasmine and Day Lily. Standing between them was Evening Primrose with a fern which she waved up and down over the queen at regular intervals as if in homage.

"Good evening, Abelia. Can I introduce my friend Erasmus to you?"

"I'm very pleased to meet you, Erasmus. May has often spoken of you."

"Good evening, Abelia. I'm very pleased to finally meet you," Erasmus said.

"Shall we go to my toadstool and talk, May. Perhaps Erasmus would like to stay with the other faeries and watch them go about their work."

This was spoken as more of a command than a suggestion.

"I'd like that, Abelia. It will be an interesting experience, I think," Erasmus said.

"Erasmus will be your responsibility, Evening Primrose. Please ensure that he is given refreshments."

"Yes, your Majesty," she said.

"Come, May, let us go." With that, they went to her toadstool to talk in private.

"So, May, you are concerned about Shasta and Merlin?" she

asked.

"Yes I am, and I miss them more than I care to admit," said May.

"I realise that," said Abelia. "Because of the concern you feel, your psychic powers are affected also."

"Yes," said May simply. "Sometimes they are quite strong, and at other times I find it very difficult."

Abelia was thoughtful for a moment and then said, "You are in love with Erasmus and this could be clouding your judgement. Be careful, May. He is a very unusual man and I can see he obviously makes you happy, but sometimes you need to look deeper for reasons. Your concern for Shasta and Merlin is unfounded, though. At the moment Shasta has come into contact with Merlin and they are getting to know one another. They are living out their previous life as she planned before she left here. Realistically it may seem strange but they are living with you, May, as you were two hundred years ago. She is no longer aware of what has happened in this life, but eventually she will remember. Time is on her side and it will all work out, I promise you".

May accepted this without question but was confused by Abelia telling her to look deeper for reasons for her power loss. Abelia was usually quite forthright. Putting this to one side, she took the opportunity to ask Abelia if she could bring her sister, Iris, and George to visit.

"Please do, May. I'll be pleased to meet them. I have to admit I am surprised at how quickly your sister has settled into Shasta. I did think you would have a few problems."

May agreed with this and said she would bring them when she felt the time was right.

Realising that she had been neglecting Erasmus in her thirst for knowledge of Shasta and Merlin, May concluded her conversation with Abelia and returned outside.

Erasmus was sitting by a tree trunk waiting patiently for May. As she appeared, his face lit up.

"Do you feel more at ease now you have spoken to Abelia?" he asked.

"Yes, thank you, Erasmus, although I'm still concerned for them both. However it's time for us to leave the faery kingdom."

No sooner had she thought it than they were back in her garden again and their size had returned to normal. This was the most difficult thing to accept when she visited Abelia. After all the visits she had made, this should have been second nature to her now, but it wasn't.

"Can I get you a drink, Erasmus?" May asked as they settled into the swing seat.

"No, thank you, I am quite content to sit here with you and enjoy the moonlight," he said.

With that he very gently kissed May on the mouth, wiping out all the concerns she was feeling for Shasta and Merlin.

May kissed him back with the same gentleness.

Eventually Erasmus decided it was time to leave and they walked to the gate at the front of the cottage.

Kissing her goodbye, Erasmus said that he would visit again soon and she wasn't to worry as he was sure that things would work out well.

With that he left and made his way down into the village to his cottage, whistling softly as he went, his mind full of thoughts as he blended with the night.

When this situation was finally resolved he would ask May to marry him if to do so fitted in with his plans. Time would tell, of course, and he had all the time in the world. He let out a soft heinous cackle and carried on whistling to himself as he suddenly disappeared, leaving behind a small vapour trail.

Chapter 27

The past

As evening approached and it began to get cooler, Shasta and Merlin, like the other villagers, made their way towards the fire. In doing so they met up with May who, having satisfied her appetite for gossip and food with many of her friends, was now enjoying the warmth given off by the fire.

Mothers sat in close proximity to the young children being lulled to sleep by the warmth of the fire. Other villagers filled with food and ale began to spontaneously break out into song, enjoying the atmosphere they had created.

Shasta and Merlin joined May and sat quietly enjoying each other's company.

As Merlin turned towards Shasta, he finally admitted to himself that he was falling in love with her. This had nothing to do with the atmosphere of the village fair. He had finally accepted that from the first moment he had set eyes on her, he had been besotted with her.

Laying her head in Merlin's lap, Shasta closed her eyes and, with a deep sigh, relaxed against his body. Merlin meanwhile stroked her hair in a gentle rhythm.

May was happy and contented for them. At last Merlin had found a woman to love and, judging by Shasta's reaction, it was reciprocated.

May, in her own mind though, felt that Shasta had been brought here for a reason and hopefully it wouldn't affect their feelings for one another. *Only time will tell*, she thought.

By ten o'clock many of the villagers and their children had left and taken to their own beds. Small groups of men and women were dotted around the fire which still burnt brightly and gave off plenty of warmth for those who wished it. Villagers threw kindling onto it as the mood took them. Now and again ribald laughter could be heard as one of the local men told a joke or made a pass at a wench. This usually encouraged his prey to give a playful slap on the face for his trouble. Mostly this was all done in fun and no offence was taken, the men too full of food and beer to remonstrate, and the woman secretly flattered by the attention.

Eventually Shasta began to stir and they also decided to leave the festivities. It had been an excellent day but she suddenly felt very tired. The heat of the fire had probably contributed to this.

As they walked up towards the cottage from the village, the rain began to gently fall, refreshing them after the heat of the fire. May walked slightly in front, with Shasta and Merlin hand-in-hand following closely behind.

As they reached the cottage, May suggested Shasta might like to sit in the garden awhile before retiring for the night. Shasta considered this for a moment and decided she would, thinking to herself it would give her a little longer with Merlin. She followed May and Merlin through the side gate to the back of the cottage. Merlin made his way to the swing seat as May had expected, indicating that Shasta should sit beside him. Settled comfortably, they sat quietly absorbing the silence while May sat at the table nearby, her eyes closed, with her mind on her own thoughts.

Shasta rested her head against Merlin's shoulder and felt at peace. This was indeed a magical garden. In the rays of the moonlight she could make out fruit trees and plants all familiar to her, and the heady perfume from plants close at hand was very intoxicating.

Sensing that they might want to be alone, May rose from her seat to go inside, telling Shasta that she would see her on the morrow.

Merlin and Shasta stayed still for fear of breaking the spell that seemed to be around the garden.

Eventually Merlin felt the urge to ask Shasta what had been

troubling her earlier on.

"Can I help in any way, mistress?" he said.

"Thank you for your offer, Merlin, but I am not really sure what ails me," she said, once again reverting to the old dialect in her anguish. "When I approached the village, I felt that I had been guided here for a reason. I am convinced that you and May are part of the reason that I was brought here, but the more I think about it the more confused I become. I know that I'm very much in love with you, Merlin, and I feel this was meant to happen."

"Oh, sweet mistress, I am so happy to hear you say that. I have loved you from the moment that I set eyes on you, and if I can help in any way I will."

"Dearest, Merlin, I thank you, but for now I think I would like to sleep in my caravan. It may help me to collect my thoughts."

Rising first, Merlin put both hands out to Shasta. Taking them she stood up and they walked arm-in-arm as far as her caravan.

Kissing her goodnight, Merlin returned to the cottage.

The following days were spent getting to know one another. Whilst Merlin worked in the fields, Shasta sometimes visited him, taking him lunch which they shared. If May felt like a break from pottering in the garden, she went also. At other times Shasta wandered down to the village to mix with the local villagers and to catch up on the gossip.

As the days went by Shasta and Merlin became more and more in love and decided finally that they would marry in the following springtime.

Chapter 28

Shasta awoke as dawn was beginning to break. Unsure of what had disturbed her so early, she lay quietly until the remains of sleep finally left her. Realising that she was in her caravan, she remembered that the previous night she had got a sudden urge to sleep here again. Shasta hoped that the familiarity of the caravan might jog her memory. Shafts of light, mingled with dust specks, began to appear through the small window of the caravan, encouraging her to begin the day. She leisurely washed and dressed, then decided to go for a long walk in the forest nearby. Breakfast could wait this morning until her return. The dew on the grass around the caravan soaked her boots but she didn't mind, this was the best time of day. In Shasta's mind, she was the only person alive and the forest was hers alone. Glancing up to the trees she could see the sun beginning to shine through the branches, throwing shafts of light to the ground. Sighing deeply, she stopped from time to time to inhale the musky smell of the forest. Mother earth gave her all and asked nothing in return.

As the forest opened up to a clearing, a vixen stood guard over her two young cubs while they devoured their breakfast. Protected by their mother they were aware of Shasta but had no fear of her.

Shasta carefully approached the vixen and it began to stiffen at first with apprehension, but relaxed in acknowledgement that they meant each other no harm. Shasta carried on walking admiring the wild flowers growing here and there. The trees shaded the ground beneath her which remained damp and cool. Occasionally she picked some earth up and let it run through her fingers. Looking up into the branches of the trees, she wished the birds good morning. They seemed to her to respond. A magpie hopped in an ungainly manner past her in his haste to be away. Shasta raised an imaginary cap and saluted him, as was the usual custom for good luck, smiling to herself as she did so. Hopefully she would see his mate as one on its own usually meant sorrow, if you believed the superstition. Two together would be joy. Strangely his mate didn't seem to be about.

As she got deeper into the forest, the density of the trees gave an eerie illusion of darkness. There were no birds and there was an unusual silence surrounding her. Shasta stopped and listened. She could hear the sound of someone using an axe. Walking towards the sound she saw a young man about the age of Merlin. Watching quietly she felt rather uncomfortable spying on him. He was stripped to the waist and, from where she stood, she could see the sweat glistening on his body.

As he lifted the axe to chop the wood from the tree he had felled, she called out

"Good morning, Sir, 'tis a beautiful one, and at this time of the morning the forest is so fresh."

Startled he turned and let the axe drop down. Seeing Shasta he began to smile and, picking up his smock, he began to use it as a towel to wipe away the sweat.

Recovering himself he said, "Morning, mistress, you be about very early."

Shasta assumed him to be a local field hand. "I love the forest at any time but especially at this time of the morning when everything is so fresh and new," she said.

"Aye, it be beautiful. I was about to get a drink in my cottage just over there on the edge of the forest. Will 'ee join me?"

Although she was thirsty, Shasta hesitated, uncertain of what to do. Sensing this, the young man told her his name was Seth and, if she preferred, he would bring a drink out to her. Realising that she was probably being a bit silly, she agreed to walk to his cottage which was in easy walking distance. Instinct however told her to be wary of this good-looking young man.

As they walked towards the cottage, Seth engaged her in conversation.

"You be that foreign travelling woman everyone talks about. I don't go to the village much but I hear tell about you by the labourers that work in the fields. They say that you changed the village and made all the flowers grow by magic overnight."

"That is partly true," said Shasta. "Mostly it was the work of the villagers. They had to want change for it to happen. I just helped them along."

Shasta had been aware as she approached the cottage that obviously Seth hadn't bothered much about his small garden. It was mostly overgrown with weeds and neglected. The narrow path to the cottage was broken in places and very uneven. The cottage itself had a run down dirty look to it.

"Maybe you will help me with my garden, mistress?"

Shasta was surprised at first by his forwardness. Recovering, she said,"But this is Shasta Village. Whatever you wish for will be, Seth. If you wish to have a beautiful garden, it will happen."

Taking a step towards her he said suggestively, "Maybe you will make it happen for me. You helped everyone else."

Seth's voice seemed to have an edge to it and his manner seemed demanding.

"First perhaps we could have that drink, Seth. I'm beginning to feel very thirsty," she said softly to ease the situation.

Instantly Seth became less hostile in his manner. "Of course, mistress. I forgot me manners for a moment. Come inside the cottage."

Seth walked ahead of her and lifted the haggaday latch to the door of the cottage. Walking inside, he held the door open for her to follow.

The first impression she got was of the darkness of the room after the sunlight outside and of a dank, musty smell. The room itself was similar to May's, with the fire the dominant feature, but there the similarity ended. There was no welcoming look to this fire. it was quite bare apart from a few dead ashes. To the left of it was a wooden pallet which sufficed as a bed, with just straw for a mattress.

A wooden table, roughly constructed from tree trunks, stood under the window, with two chairs around it. Across the centre of the floor lay a threadbare rug and, in the sink, were dishes with dried food caked onto them.

Seth made no excuses for the condition of the room and took two goblets from the shelf, filling them with ginger beer.

Inviting Shasta to sit down at the table, he handed her the drink.

"I hope it be to your liking, mistress," he said.

Although it was warm, Shasta agreed it was to her taste.

Feeling the need to make conversation, she asked if he had lived in the cottage very long.

"Aye, mistress, I have lived alone here for quite a few years. It needs a woman's touch, though, and I intend to take me a wife afore so long."

"Oh, have you got someone in mind?"

All of her instincts made Shasta instantly regret the remark.

Very casually he sat upright in the chair and slid his arms to rest on the table. With a sickly grin on his face, and looking Shasta straight in the eyes, he said with great emphasis, "Oh yes, mistress, I have met just the woman."

Shasta chose to ignore the insinuation and, finishing the last of her drink, thanked him for the refreshment. She rose from the table and said it was time she made her way back.

"Maybe you will visit again soon, mistress?" Seth asked.

"If I am walking this way again I will certainly call on you, Seth," she said, knowing very well that she would try and avoid it at all costs.

They left the cottage and Seth walked as far as the edge of the forest with her, seemingly preoccupied with his own thoughts. Picking up his axe he continued with his work as Shasta made her way back through the forest.

As she walked she began to assimilate her feelings.

Seth was a very good-looking young man, not many years older than her, she supposed. She couldn't deny that he had a body that any young maiden would be pleased to look at with pleasure.

Suddenly a mental image of Merlin invaded her thoughts. Why was she even thinking about Seth when she had her beloved Merlin? Her footsteps became lighter and she began to hum to herself as she made her way back through the forest and into the sunlight again.

Her stomach grumbled, reminding her that she still hadn't eaten, but she felt light of heart and she couldn't wait to see Merlin again.

Chapter 29

Merlin had also woken early. He was eager to see Shasta before he started work in the fields. He stood outside her caravan in a quandary. He had called to her and, getting no reply, finally looked inside, disappointed to find it empty. There was no sign of her anywhere. He decided to walk down to the small stream at the edge of the forest but she wasn't there either. He sat there for a while watching the shallow stream as it meandered over flat rocks and glistened in the sun. Many times he had used them as stepping-stones to get to the other side. Sometimes, due to his haste, he had also got wet feet where he had misjudged his step.

Merlin watched the reflection of the sun on the slow moving water and it made him feel lazy. He lay back on the grass, closed his eyes, and folded his arms behind his head. His thoughts drifted towards Shasta and he relished the happiness that she had brought him. He had never been so happy. This was the first woman he had ever loved and he imagined he heard Shasta calling his name. It seemed very real and he opened his eyes. He was blinded at first by the brightness of the sun and then he saw her running towards him. As he stood up she rapidly closed the distance between them.

Merlin drank in her beauty and gathered her to him, pulling her close. He kissed her with a passion that surprised both of them and left them breathless.

Pulling apart he said, "Mistress, I searched for you and was concerned when I couldn't find you."

"Oh, my beloved, I woke early and decided to take a walk in the forest, it was so beautiful and peaceful."

"If I had known I would have walked with you to keep you company," said Merlin.

"Oh, I had company," she said. "When I reached the edge of the forest, I met a woodcutter called Seth. We exchanged a few pleasantries and he offered me a drink in his cottage, which I accepted."

For the first time Merlin felt jealousy. He knew Seth very well from evenings spent in the local tavern. Seth was the local lushington, or drunkard, who regularly got into fights with other men for paying too much attention to their wives. Due to his good looks and strong physique he was frequently found in their beds in a drunken stupor by their men folk. On occasions he even took a local doxey or woman of low repute. It was also common knowledge that he was looking for a wife to take to his bed.

He was not at all popular among the men of the village and, on the whole, the women just used him out of pure lust.

Merlin didn't know whether to share this with Shasta but he didn't want to give her too much cause for worry. Eventually he said, "Be mindful of Seth, Mistress. I have known him a long time and he is not all he seems."

"Why, Merlin, do I detect a note of jealousy in your voice?" Shasta asked.

"I love you more than my own life, Shasta. I wouldn't like to see you hurt in any way, but I do not deny that I am jealous of him spending time with you."

"Beloved Merlin, you have nothing to fear. You will always be my only love."

Taking his hand in hers, Shasta pulled him close and kissed him tenderly. Then, putting her arm through his, they walked back towards her caravan.

Realising how hungry she was, Shasta asked Merlin to join her for breakfast.

Accepting that he would probably be late joining the other labourers in the fields, he felt that breakfasting with Shasta would be worth it.

As they reached the caravan they could see May in the garden pottering among her flowers, as usual. Shasta called out to her.

Turning, she waved to them both and made her way towards the gate.

"Good morning and how are you both this fine morning?"

"Very well thank you, May. We are just about to have breakfast. Will you join us?"

At first May declined, thinking she would leave the young ones alone, but both Shasta and Merlin persuaded her to join them.

They decided to sit outside the caravan to eat as it was such a beautiful morning. Over breakfast Shasta told May about meeting Seth in the forest. For an instant May's face clouded over. This didn't go unnoticed.

"That one be trouble mistress," said May, reverting to the old dialect. Shasta noticed that this happened with all of the villagers from time to time, but mostly when they were excited or angry, regardless of their position in the community.

"He causes more trouble in the village during one night in the tavern than all the men on a Saturday night drinking spree," said May with much emphasis on the word 'he'. "You would be well advised to stay away from him," She continued.

Shasta had never heard a harsh word come from May until now and it disturbed her greatly. A feeling of foreboding came over her and, having finished their breakfast, she collected the dishes to take them inside the caravan for something to do. May stood up and, making her excuses, returned to her garden.

Merlin, already late for his work, said goodbye to Shasta and hoped that they would share Nuncheon together at midday. She promised that she would prepare some food, or bait as the field workers called it, and agreed to meet him.

Chapter 30

Shasta picked up her black cooking pot and sprinkled a few fresh herbs into it as the mood took her, including plenty of sage as it helped her think more clearly. She then picked up her three-legged stool and, leaving her caravan, made her way to the edge of the forest, needing to be alone with her thoughts.

Finding a secluded spot under a large oak tree, she set her pot and stool down close to the trunk of the tree. She collected some nearby bits of kindling wood, made a small fire with practised ease and stood the cooking pot on top. Sitting on her stool, she began to meditate by staring into the pot and inhaling the pungent odour of the herbs as they began to spit and sizzle. Breathing deeply she felt the familiar light-headedness and her thoughts began to drift. She went back in time and relived everything that had happened since she had come to the village.

Her thoughts took her back to Beth and the ritual they had performed deep in the forest for Weodmonath. Although she had seen this tradition performed in another village, she felt convinced that she had performed it herself on another occasion. The village fayre had been very lively and the villagers had made it the success it was.

Her thoughts then turned to May. Their friendship, although relatively new, had become even stronger of late and she felt as if they had always known each other. Their love for Merlin was mutual. May loved him as a son, while Shasta was in love with him body and soul, and when the spring came they would be wed.

As this thought passed through her mind she reached down and picked some wild mushrooms growing within arms reach and threw them into the pot. Perhaps the combined aromas would clear her head. Her psychic ability seemed to have deserted her of late just when she needed it more than ever, either that or a faery godmother, she thought with amusement.

As she uttered these words an apparition appeared before her. Shasta accepted this with no surprise. It wasn't the first time she had seen apparitions during meditation, the difference this time being that the face she was looking upon was perfectly beautiful.

"Who are you?" she asked.

"My name is Abelia and I am the Faery Queen."

"The name is familiar to me but I can't think why," said Shasta.

"I promise you that you will remember everything in time, Shasta, when the time is right."

As Shasta was about to question her further, the apparition slowly disappeared into a mist that had risen from the pot. Then everything was as it was before.

Shasta was now more confused than ever. Why couldn't she recall the name? It was obviously very important and connected to her reason for being here in the village. As she sat looking into the pot, the scene changed again. This time she was looking at herself. Her features were the same but her clothes were all wrong. Her hair was in a plait as she usually wore it, but she was wearing a brightly coloured dress that she didn't recognise and which only came to her knees. She also looked much younger. How very strange, she thought.

Next she saw May, but she looked older than she was now. Although she was dressed very similarly to her current fashion, the kitchen table she sat at looked nothing like the one in her cottage. It was of a much lighter, shiny wood and the legs had unusual carvings on them. The four chairs also had carvings which matched the table. Lying in a large wicker chair near the table was a black cat completely surrounded by cushions, and resting between its front paws was a rag doll with long blonde plaits dressed in dungarees.

"Primrose!" exclaimed Shasta.

Seeing her doll had triggered her memory... Oh how much she loved Primrose. It had been given to her by her mothers' sister when she had been born and it had been everywhere with her.

Slowly it all came back to her. She now knew that she had come back here to save Merlin's life.

Shasta needed to talk to May. Picking up her cooking pot, which had cooled during the apparitions, she ran back to her caravan. Leaving the cooking pot outside by the steps, she hurried up the path to May's garden. Sensing that she was in the back garden she hurried through the gate calling her name as she went.

May had been lounging in her swing seat, but hearing the urgency in Shasta's' voice rose and met her.

"Mistress Shasta, what ails thee?"

"May, dearest Aunt May, I now know why I came to the village," she said breathlessly.

"Sit down here, mistress, and I will get us a drink."

Summoning up two goblets of ale, May handed one to Shasta and sat beside her.

Shasta took a long drink to quench her thirst and began to tell May about the apparitions she had seen. May didn't interrupt until the story was finished.

Breathless from excitement, Shasta began to try to explain to May. Although she was here in the village of Shasta now, she had actually been born two hundred years in the future, returning to this life to right a wrong.

May, who accepted most things on face value, looked confused.

Shasta, seeing this, started again.

"In two hundred years from now in this village, I will begin another life as a young girl called Summer. My parents will be Iris and George Backer and my mothers' sister will be called May. When I am eight and a half years old, my mother will arrange for me to stay with my Aunt May.

She will have sole charge of me during this time, and because my skin burns very easily in the sun she will change my hair to blonde.

Aunt May will then explain to me about Shasta village being

149

named after me and, because of the magical qualities of Shasta, I will age to a young woman within a matter of weeks. She will also tell me that she has faeries at the bottom of her garden and invite me to visit Abelia, the faery queen. Both May and Abelia will tell me about my past life, which is in fact the life I am now living at the moment with you and Merlin. Everything I do in this life will affect my new life in the future. I realise it must be hard for you to understand May. To come back to this lifetime is possibly fraught with danger for me because I am trying to change the future, but I was prepared to take that risk to save Merlin's life."

May instantly became fearful for Merlin, and the anguish showed on her face.

"I don't understand, mistress. Why is Merlin's life in danger?"

"I also learnt that I will have another suitor for my hand in marriage and, because of my love for Merlin, I will reject him. In a jealous rage he will kill Merlin or mutilate him in some way, and that is why I have to come back in time to try to rearrange things," said Shasta. "My problem is I don't know who he is yet. It may be Seth, of course, but I have to be sure first," she said wistfully. "I promised Merlin that I would prepare some bait for him and meet him for nuncheon. Please don't relate any of this to him, May, until I am sure" begged Shasta.

"Of course not, mistress, but I am fearful for his life, as you are," she said.

Leaving May to think about everything she had been told, Shasta went back to her caravan and prepared nuncheon for her and Merlin. When it was ready, she walked the well-trodden path used by the labourers to the fields.

As she reached the cross stile gate, Shasta balanced her basket on the top and leant on it. She watched the labourers in the distance using their pitchforks with practised expertise. Seeing Merlin on top of a hayrick, she laughed to herself as he started to clown around, much to the amusement of the other workers. This was a side of

Merlin that so far she hadn't seen much of, and she enjoyed watching him, knowing that he wasn't aware of it.

Eventually he jumped down off of the hayrick. Shasta climbed the gate and walked towards him, calling his name as she did so. At first he didn't hear her but, on the second time, he turned. Seeing Shasta, he ran towards her and lifted her into the air, swinging her around until she was as breathless as him.

"Merlin, please put me down. You're making me dizzy," she said, laughing happily.

As Merlin lowered her to the ground, he took the basket from her hand and they walked towards one of the hayricks to eat.

Eventually the other field hands stopped their work and joined them, telling Shasta of the antics that Merlin got up to to keep them amused. This endeared her to Merlin all the more. It firmed her resolve to make sure that she saved Merlin before anything happened to him. Obviously he was very popular with the local field hands and she felt comforted by this. If necessary she felt that she could call on them for help.

When they had finished eating, Shasta lay back and enjoyed the heat of the sun on her face. Merlin sat watching her once again, unable to believe how lucky he was to have her. Many of the local men had stated the same thing to him during one of his infrequent visits to the local tavern. Mostly they spoke of Shasta with reverence.

Unbeknown to Merlin, Seth in one of his drunken stupors had also spoken of Shasta, but in a very derogatory fashion, which had been frowned upon by all that had heard him. He had been bragging about her visit to his cottage, deliberately taking away the innocence of the visit, and intimating that he intended to ask Shasta to walk out with him at the next opportunity he had.

Reluctant to disturb her, but needing to restart his work, Merlin bent over Shasta and gently kissed her. Her eyes flew open and she kissed him back.

"I have to restart work, mistress," he said with reluctance.

Sighing deeply at the thought of leaving him again, she rose to her feet. Kissing him farewell she watched as he joined the other workers. With a final wave she picked up the basket and began to make her way back to her caravan, deciding that she would join May in her garden if she were there.

Chapter 31

May was sitting in her swing seat by the back door of the cottage. She had eaten her lunch and was beginning to feel slightly lonely.

She had started to get used to Shasta joining her for lunch. Sometimes, for a change, they had lunch in the village by the green, then slowly walked back together arm-in-arm. She would just have to get used to the idea that she would probably be doing more things on her own now. She was very happy for them both but the news Shasta had shared with her had disturbed her greatly. Her natural instinct was to protect Merlin but there was only so much that she could do.

She rose from the swing seat, stretching her body as she did so, and slowly walked down through the garden. As always the flowers gave her so much pleasure. She could happily spend all day just admiring them and making up her potions for the local villagers depending on their requirements. Her knowledge had come from an old woman that had lived on the edge of the forest in a caravan not dissimilar to Shasta's. She had come across the woman quite by chance and had stopped to pass the time of day with her. They had exchanged ideas about various herbs and mushrooms and, putting their ideas together, they had come up with cures for many ailments.

As she passed the sweet peas and honeysuckle she inhaled their heady intoxicating perfume. The beautiful red roses also demanded her attention and, holding their blooms in her hand, she praised each one. They in turn lowered their heads in shyness of her praise as she released them.

Unconsciously she had made her way towards the wishing well. Perhaps Abelia was drawing her near and maybe it was time that Shasta visited her in this lifetime. As all these thoughts passed through her mind, she heard Shasta calling out to her.

"I'm here, mistress" she called back and made her way to the cottage, deliberately walking on some herbs growing at ground level to release their aroma.

Reaching Shasta, she took in the contented look on her face. It gave her such pleasure to see her and Merlin so happy and in love.

"I think, mistress Shasta, that I have never seen you happier than at this moment."

"Oh, May, I have never felt happier. I'm so pleased that I decided to come to this village. Fate was certainly on my side. I didn't know it at the time, but now of course I know that it was meant to be."

Chapter 32

Erasmus sat alone as usual in his cottage. It was sparsely furnished but there was sufficient for his needs. He didn't make a habit of encouraging visitors, preferring to remain alone with his thoughts.

He stood quietly in front of his book of spells which was normally invisible to any unexpected prying eyes. By waving his hand over the table, the book appeared.

Having lived many lifetimes, (he gave up counting long ago how many there were), he had used his spell book many times. Through the years, he had perfected the art of mentally transporting his body and thoughts at will to any era of time.

He gave a satisfied throaty cackle and thought about his recent misdemeanours. He had used his spells to vandalise the garden centre belonging to May's brother-in-law. That had been the easiest of all and it had also brought Shasta to May. Yes, he could have brought her there anyway by mere thoughts, but that was only half the fun.

He had this lifetime to fill and there were many years still ahead of him, so why do good deeds when he could meddle in others' lives to his own advantage? If he was honest, his powers made things too easy for him. Sometimes he preferred to act just like any other mortal.

When Shasta and May had been limited in their powers, this had been his doing. No problem for him at all, when he only had to block or close their channel of thoughts. It was so easy to plant an idea to his advantage and play with their minds. Unbeknown to them, he was completely in control as and when it suited him.

Abelia was more of a problem as he had realised what she was capable of when he visited the faery kingdom. Several times he had tentatively tested his powers on her but on most occasions she had proven to be stronger. This didn't bother him too much, however, because the ultimate outcome had already been planned and meticulously worked out.

Vengeance would be his without a doubt.

May had become very useful to him, and a means to an end. During all his lives, he had mostly steered clear of women, only using them for his own ends. May was different, though, and he had become quite fond of her. He had given her a love token for her hair which she wore consistently. He would try to ensure that she didn't get hurt but, if necessary, she would have to be sacrificed to achieve his goal.

Merlin was wary of him, of course, and he knew that. Fortunately his present body bore no resemblance to Merlin's old master in his previous life. Erasmus in that life time as his master had ensured that the spell went wrong and Merlin had stayed a cat, but he had paid dearly for it.

Erasmus had then begun his plans, knowing that it would perhaps take a couple of hundred years to achieve his goal, but his quarry was worth it, and what was a couple of hundred years when he could gain the sweetest prize of all for all eternity?

Chapter 33

The present

George had woken very early and turned to look at his wife who was still sleeping. She was lying on her back with one arm thrown above her head, her hair entangled around it as if she had been playing with it during her dreams.

He was still very much in love with her even though she exasperated him at times. Since being in Shasta she had mellowed beyond recognition and, in a way, was becoming more like May every day. Instead of wearing her hair neatly pinned up, she had taken to wearing it in a plait in the style of May and it suited her face. Here in Shasta it had grown at a remarkable rate.

In need of a drink, he gradually eased himself towards the edge of the bed. Iris turned towards him and threw her arm across his chest possessively. Waiting a couple of seconds until he was sure she was still asleep, he gradually removed it and slid out of the bed.

Quietly he gathered up his dressing gown, which he put on, and made his way to the kitchen. Yes, he could very easily have just wished for a drink and it would have appeared, but sometimes it was still nice to do things the old fashioned way, except that May didn't possess a kettle. As he passed her bedroom on the way to the kitchen he could see her lying in her bed still asleep, which was rather unusual.

He sat at the table and decided to give in to laziness by thinking of a cup of steaming coffee and instantly it was there in front of him.

As he sipped the steaming brew, he watched the sun starting to rise whilst enjoying the early dawn chorus. In the distance he thought he saw someone that looked remarkably like Erasmus. Assuming it was the light playing tricks, he put the thought to one side. Erasmus couldn't get into the garden without coming through the gate, and if he had he would have heard him. Looking again he was convinced that someone was there so, opening the door, he began to walk through the garden. As he got closer, the shape began to disappear. Although he knew that many strange things happened in Shasta, he was reluctant to believe that someone was capable of materialising out of nothing and dematerialising again in this day and age. At first he was startled and just stared as if in a dream. Then reality took over and he began to believe that probably it was all his imagination anyway. As he turned round towards the kitchen, he heard a very soft cackling sound behind him. Momentarily he hesitated, but rather than turn round, he quickened his step toward the kitchen. He decided against mentioning the experience to May or Iris. There would be no point in frightening them because his mind was playing tricks, and he convinced himself that it was.

Whistling to himself for reassurance, he returned to the kitchen.

Erasmus, in his state of invisibility, smiled to himself. He loved playing mind games and, with that thought, he transported himself instantly back to his cottage.

George returned to the kitchen table and carried on with his coffee as if nothing had happened. By now the sun had completely risen and shafts of sunlight could be seen through the trees in the distance of May's garden. It was the start of another beautiful day in Shasta.

"Good morning, George dear, what a beautiful morning." Iris put her arms round her husband's neck lovingly.

"Good morning, Iris. I didn't hear you come up behind me" he said.

"You seemed to be miles away. are you all right?" she asked softly.

"Yes, I'm fine, Iris. I was just enjoying the beautiful morning."

Iris sat down beside him and imagined a cup of Earl Grey tea and it appeared. Placing her hands round the cup to warm them, she began to sip the hot liquid.

"May seems to be having a long lay in this morning. She's still asleep which is unusual for her. She is always such an early riser. Perhaps all the early mornings have caught up with her finally. Would you care for some toast, George? I'm having some"

"Yes, please, Iris. Two slices, please."

For Iris the novelty of magic still hadn't worn off. As they sat eating their breakfast, May appeared at the kitchen door. Still in a dressing gown, she sat at the table alongside them, mumbling a sleepy good morning. A cup of coffee appeared in front of her along with a slice of toast and marmalade.

"I was having the strangest dream," she said as she sipped the hot coffee. "I dreamt that Erasmus was in the garden calling to me but I couldn't wake up to answer him. Each time I tried to open my eyes he seemed to disappear in a puff of smoke."

George choked on his coffee. So what was going on here exactly, he wondered. It seemed that May had experienced in a dream what he had seen in the garden. Maybe he didn't imagine it after all. Oh Lord, he thought again, what is going on?

He choked again because Iris was thumping him on the back.

"Are you alright, George?" she asked.

"I will be, woman, if you stop thumping my back."

"Sorry, George, I thought it would help," she said

George decided to hold his own counsel until he could speak to May without Iris being there. Something felt very wrong; maybe his first impression of Erasmus had been correct after all. Still he wouldn't make any hasty judgements and upset May. He was far too fond of her.

"Perhaps later this morning we could walk to the village?" inquired Iris.

"Then tonight we could go to Faery Cove and meet Abelia," said May

"I think that's a lovely idea, May," said George. He had already told Iris about Faery Cove and Abelia. Amazingly she had again taken it in her stride, surprising him yet further with her adaptability.

They walked at a leisurely pace to the village, and then passed the time quenching their thirst and talking to the local villagers who had got used to them being with May. Some of the locals made requests of May for potions. Previously made orders were also passed out. Iris was fascinated by this and asked if she could help with the next batch of potions to be made up, which May readily agreed to. George could occupy himself in the garden.

May and Iris spent an enjoyable afternoon making up the villagers' requests. Iris having a natural aptitude for it, timidly suggested ideas to May which she agreed to try. As her confidence grew, Iris began to experiment with her own ideas, including an aphrodisiac for George which amused May immensely. She rather liked her 'new' sister. Iris would include the aphrodisiac in his evening meal which tonight they decided to cook in the 'old fashioned' conventional way, with maybe a little bit of magic just to speed things up. Chicken and potatoes were decided upon, and neither of them particularly wanted to peel the potatoes.

As they sat at the kitchen table they talked over old times from their childhood which bonded them together more closely. George had been told to stay in the garden until the meal was ready and had been bribed by Iris with a concessionary beer, much to his delight.

As the meal was divided into portions, Iris added the aphrodisiac to George's meal while May kept watch for him.

Calling George in from the garden, the three sat down to enjoy the meal. Finishing every last morsel on his plate, George concurred it was the best meal he had tasted so far in Shasta. Iris and May just smiled conspiratorially.

They rested in the garden for a while as the evening drew to a close and gentle rain began to fall. As usual the flowers raised their heads and drank greedily. Iris and George still marvelled at the way they could sit in a shower of rain and not get wet.

"I think it's time to visit Faery Cove" said May quietly. "Are you ready?"

"Definitely," said Iris.

Rising, they made their way by the moonlight to the gate at the far end of the garden. May gave them instructions about drinking from the cup attached to the well. Allowing them to drink first, she was able to witness first hand their experience of shrinking in size. Quickly she joined them, explaining that they were still in her garden but obviously everything seemed different to their diminished size. Iris grabbed George's hand for comfort and reassurance as they slowly followed May. Just in the distance was a ring of light which seemed to be swaying about. May walking slightly ahead and called to Princess Evening Primrose, explaining that finally she had brought her sister, Iris, and brother-in-law, George, to visit Abelia.

Probably for the first time in their lives, George and Iris were speechless. This was the stuff of pure fantasy and, if truth be known, they were enjoying the experience. The faeries walked in their splendour in front of them, carrying their lanterns lit by tiny glow worms to light the way to the faery kingdom.

Abelia sat on her throne waiting for them to arrive. She always enjoyed seeing May and was pleased to be meeting her family. She wasn't exactly too sure about Erasmus. He seemed to be mentally challenging her on his visit and that hadn't happened to her for at least a couple of hundred years. She had got the better of him, of course, but it had disturbed her.

Hearing the soft singing of the faeries as they approached her, she once again composed herself and was smiling with anticipation by the time they all arrived.

"Welcome, May," she said warmly.

"Hello, Abelia, can I present you to my sister, Iris, and her husband, George?"

Hearing this, Iris did an awkward curtsey, still trying to get used to her size and the fact that her clothes had also shrunk along with the rest of her. George attempted a sort of bow from the waist, unsure really what he was supposed to do.

"I'm very pleased to meet you both. Please relax, there is no ceremony here for visitors."

Iris stared at the pretty queen dressed in silver and gold. She seemed to sparkle from her head to the soft gold and silver slippers on her feet.

"May I say what a pleasure it is to meet a faery queen" said George, giving Iris time to regain her composure.

"Indeed," said Iris, now playing the whole situation as if it was second nature to her.

"We shall retire to my toadstool for refreshments. Faeries, please go about your business", said Abelia.

When they were settled and refreshed with a drink, Iris asked what exactly the faeries did.

"Each of them has designated jobs to do, Iris. Some ensure that the spiders have enough silk to spin their webs. Sometimes this is then draped over the delicate flowers at night. Others tend the flowers to ensure they don't get burnt by the sun. The ferns mostly keep them cool, but sometimes a flower will have a will of its own. The flowers usually have their faces turned up to the sun so that the bees can easily collect the pollen. Sometimes they become a bit shy by nightfall and my faeries help the bees. This all has to be done at night as, by tradition, faeries never appear in the daytime." Both Iris and George sat listening intently but eventually Iris felt tiredness creeping over her and stifled a yawn.

"Maybe that is long enough for a first visit," said Abelia. "Perhaps you would like to visit again."

"That would be lovely, Abelia," said Iris with sincerity.

George helped Iris to her feet and they turned to leave.

"Before you go, May, I should like a word, please," said Abelia.

"We'll wait outside, May," said George.

"Have you seen Erasmus lately, May?" asked Abelia when they

were alone.

Explaining that she hadn't, May related the recent dream and the fact that it had concerned her; also that her past dreams had never interfered with her ability to rise with the dawn.

"I am aware that you have very strong feelings for him, May, but be careful," warned Abelia again in a kindly tone.

"Thank you. I will heed your warning."

Both women had a mutual respect for one another, but May was in love with Erasmus and that could easily cloud her judgement.

Walking outside with Abelia, she bade her farewell and allowed herself, George and Iris to be escorted back to the edge of the garden by the faeries.

As they reached the gate, May wished them back to their normal size and so it was. Although Iris accepted May's explanation, it was still a lot to take in when one wasn't used to it. Right now, though, she was more interested in her bed and to test her experiment with the powers of the aphrodisiac she had made earlier for George!

Chapter 34

The past

Shasta lay on her bed in the cool of her caravan. Sometimes she preferred to be alone with her thoughts even though they had made room for her to sleep in the cottage. Through the open door she could smell the earthy floor of the forest, mostly damp under the surrounding pine trees but in other places baked hard, each part having its own individual smell.

As she lay there, her thoughts were reflected by the myriad of colours in the interior of the caravan. Many other thoughts went through her mind, including why her powers were sometimes blocked which was an unusual occurrence in itself. It had never happened before but it had happened several times since she had come to the village. It was almost as if they were being slowly drained from her. She did sometimes wonder if May was having the same problem as she also occasionally found it difficult to focus. Who would have an equal or stronger power than her? Whoever it was, if indeed there was someone, they would be extremely powerful.

Maybe she should talk to May about it.

Having made the decision, she sat up and slid off the bed. She had intended to stay there for some time but this was far more important.

It really was convenient having two homes in such close proximity to each other. Going into May's garden she noticed that the back door to the kitchen was closed. Maybe May was down in the village.

She entered the cottage and called out but there was no one about. Merlin was still working in the fields. Obviously May was in the village and yet she felt that the cottage was occupied. Walking through the kitchen, she felt a presence over by the fireplace. The black cooking pot was in its usual place hanging over the fire, slowly preparing their meal for the evening. Shasta was still convinced though there was someone in the cottage. Glancing around the main room she saw no one, but she felt watched. Suddenly she heard the most grotesque laugh, and yet it wasn't a laugh, more of a cackle. Her hand flew to her throat and she turned and fled through the kitchen door straight into May.

"Child, whatever ails thee? she asked.

"Oh, May, I came to find you to talk to you and when I came into the cottage, I realised that you were probably in the village but I felt that there was a presence here. Then suddenly I heard this grotesque cackle, it was horrible." Shasta let this all out in one breath.

May, visibly shocked that this had happened in her cottage, sat on the nearest chair to hand, urging Shasta to do likewise.

"Calm yourself, Shasta," she said without much conviction. "Merlin will be back soon. We can talk this over with him. In the meantime I will mix up a potion for you to take."

Having mixed the ingredients together, May gave Shasta the potion to drink and sat beside her again.

"Thank you, May. I am beginning to feel a little bit calmer now. I don't know what came over me."

May was reluctant to admit it, but she had also felt a presence in the cottage from time to time of late, but never when Merlin was there. She decided not to tell Shasta yet as she didn't want to frighten her away. Merlin would be devastated if she left the village.

Shasta suggested that they take a walk in the forest, feeling a need to be in open spaces once again. May agreed and gathered up a few bits in a basket for them to eat once inside the forest.

As they walked, they began to relax and pointed out various things to one another. Shasta started to laugh as she enjoyed the squirrels digging for nuts, whilst May showed her various types of mushrooms growing in profusion. Both women were at one with nature.

By mutual consent they sat in a clearing by a fine old oak tree. Its branches sheltered them from the heat of the sun. May took the bread and cake from the basket and they ate in a companionable silence.

Here in the forest Shasta felt at peace; nothing could touch her here. Yet she could not shake the feeling that someone was still watching her, but from the distance.

She watched May from the corner of her eye, noticing that she didn't seem quite so relaxed as usual.

Eventually Shasta asked May if she had had a similar experience to hers. May was silent for a moment and then admitted that she had experienced something similar recently, and her powers of clairvoyance didn't seem as strong recently. They both agreed it was rather unnerving.

Shasta heard whistling coming from behind her and, turning round, she saw Seth approaching them. He carried his axe over his shoulder in a casual way and his body glistened with sweat.

"Good day, mistress," he called to May who looked at him with disdain but mumbled a slightly audible, "Good day".

"Good day, mistress Shasta. T'is a fine day for a picnic. May I join you for a moment?" he asked in a more subservient tone than on their last meeting, his accent seemingly far more refined, which surprised Shasta but she decided not to comment.

"Please do, Seth," she said, much to the obvious disgust of May who had deliberately turned herself away.

"Are you well?" Shasta asked. "You look as if you have been working hard."

"Indeed, mistress, I have chopped a tree and it is now in many logs awaiting the fire," he said with some pride.

Shasta looked to the distance unsure of what to say. May had made her opinion of him very clear and this was being reinforced now. Maybe he wasn't as bad as the folk in the village thought.

"You seem thoughtful, mistress Shasta. Can I help in any way?"

"It's very kind of you, Seth, but it is something that I have to deal with myself," she said.

"Very well, mistress, but if you need someone to talk to, I will listen even if I can't help. I am usually at my cottage."

"Thank you, Seth, I will remember."

He stood up, picked up his axe which he rested back on his shoulder, and carried on walking through the forest in the direction they had come from.

One minute he was in full view, and suddenly he was no longer there. *How strange*, thought Shasta, but then let the thought slip from her mind.

"That one is trouble, mistress, for all his fine words," May said, breaking the silence.

"Maybe he is trying to change his ways," said Shasta.

"Don't be misguided by his fancy words, mistress" she persisted.

"Thank you for your concern, May. I will be careful."

Rising, Shasta took hold of May's hands to help her up and completely misjudged her balance, falling back down again on top of May. Laughing together - which broke the tension - they stood up, collected the basket, and made their way back out of the forest towards the cottage.

As they approached the cottage they could see Merlin making his way inside. Shasta called out to him and, turning round, he ran back to greet her by sweeping her off of her feet and swinging her around which he did frequently of late. This was much to May's amusement as he had always done this to her before Shasta arrived in the village.

Once inside, May set about dishing up their meal whilst Shasta related her earlier experience in the cottage.

With concern he reconfirmed that she had recovered herself, but also stated that he hadn't been aware of feeling anything untoward in the cottage.

After their meal Shasta and Merlin went to the caravan while May began to harvest the lavender ready to put into muslin bags. Sometimes she gave them away on a whim, whilst other times she decorated them with bows and ribbons and sold them cheaply at the local market or fair. As they were always in demand, May always grew extra shrubs. Consequently the lavender took longer to harvest, but she didn't mind as the ethos of the village was to help all of one's neighbours. Sometimes she made her own jams and sold them, but equally she bought them from local neighbours. Frequently items such as these were bartered for and many different types of produce exchanged hands if there was a shortage of money.

As the evening wore on, Shasta told Merlin that she was extremely tired and needed to sleep. Merlin would have preferred to stay longer but accepted that she had had a long and tiring day, and returned to the cottage to find May.

Shasta found it very difficult to sleep with all the events of the day flooding back into her mind. As she thought about them over and over again, trying to make some sense of them, her eyes finally started to close. Her last thoughts before sleep overtook her were of Seth walking through the forest and disappearing. Why was he walking toward May's cottage when he lived in the opposite direction? He could have been walking to the village, of course, but there was a short cut very near to his cottage, and why had he disappeared from view so suddenly?

As she fell into a troubled sleep, she saw Merlin's face in front of her eyes. Suddenly Seth was there. His face seemed to be split into two. One half she recognised as his, but the other side was of a more mature man with large haunting eyes. Shasta woke again in a cold sweat. The moonlight was streaming in through the caravan door which normally she did not bother to shut as she always felt safe in the village. Shasta decided to make herself a drink as she obviously wasn't going to get any sleep for a while. As she drank the calming liquid she thought about the fact that she had been dreaming of Seth. She loved Merlin deeply, so why was she thinking about Seth in this way and what did the split face signify? This puzzled her as usually she had answers to her dreams and the second face she didn't recognise at all.

She would talk it over with May and Merlin in the morning. Feeling calmer after her drink, she got back into bed and fell into a dreamless sleep this time. When she awoke the sun was streaming in through the caravan door.

Instead of going to the cottage to have breakfast, as she had been doing recently Shasta, decided to walk in the forest again. Not only did it give her such pleasure to be surrounded by nature, but the walk would enable her to clear her mind of her strange dream.

As she walked, her mind wandered yet again to her feelings for Merlin. Although she loved him dearly, Seth came into her thoughts more and more lately although she didn't want to admit it. Without realising it, she had reached the clearing. His cottage was in view but, even more strangely, he was working in his garden and he had obviously been doing it for a while because the flowers were beautiful. Shasta village was obviously once again working its magic. The cottage from the distance also seemed different, somehow cleaner looking. As she got closer, the overall change in the cottage was obvious. Seth was making an effort to impress someone.

"Good morning, Seth," Shasta called out to him.

Standing upright he waved as he recognised her.

"Good morning, mistress Shasta, it's a beautiful morning. Would you care to have breakfast with me this morning?"

Without thinking about it she agreed. Opening the haggaday latch for her, he allowed her to precede him into the cottage whilst he followed behind. Instantly she noted the change to the interior. It was as if it had received a woman's touch. Everything was clean and very tidy, and she commented on it.

"If I am looking for a wife, I have to show that I can offer them some comforts even if I am just a wood cutter. You were right, mistress, if you think pleasant thoughts they will happen. I was jealous of everything that was happening in the village and I felt excluded, but now I have made an effort, the local villagers have been more helpful to me."

Whilst they breakfasted, Shasta and Seth talked about village life and how it had changed of late. Shasta couldn't help but reflect on how different Seth seemed to be, somehow more appealing and, after all, he was an extremely good looking young man. He would be a fine catch for the right woman.

Having finished their light breakfast, Shasta thanked him as she rose to leave. Seth tried to persuade her to stay awhile but she explained that she had to get back to see Merlin before he left for work in the fields. For a second Seth's face showed a frown but as Shasta registered the change it instantly became neutral, as before.

"Tell me, Seth, are you courting one of the village maidens yet?" Shasta asked him, keeping the conversation light again.

"Not yet, mistress, but I have got my eye on someone. Unfortunately she is walking out with someone else."

As he said this, he moved slowly towards Shasta who was finding it difficult to move away. As he put his hands to her face, she realised she had become powerless to resist. His eyes were almost hypnotic and she felt out of control. As his head came closer to hers, she expectantly put her mouth forward to receive his kiss and closed her eyes. As he kissed her mouth her whole body yielded to him.

If she had not closed her eyes, she would have seen his face change completely as Erasmus took over Seth's body.

At last, he thought, *I have her*, but he knew that this was only the beginning and allowed Seth's body to take over from his once again.

His time was not yet, but he could bend Shasta to his will on demand. He had just proved it.

Seth was first to move away surprised at Shasta's reaction. It felt as if she had melted against him. She was in love with Merlin, wasn't she? Could he really stand a chance with her? What had happened to him? He was left feeling drained and weak. This was a new experience for him.

"Please forgive me, mistress, I didn't mean to take advantage in that way," he said putting distance between them.

"I'm sorry too, Seth. I don't know what came over me." Embarrassed she backed towards the door.

"Thank you for breakfast. I have to go."

With that she opened the door and ran back towards the forest to gather her thoughts.

Breathless, Shasta finally stopped running as she reached the deepest part.

How could she have let that happen?

She had been powerless to stop it. Though. it was as if someone had taken over her body and gradually drawn her towards Seth. Nevertheless, she had enjoyed the kiss; it was like nothing she had experienced before.

When Merlin kissed her it was with a gentle passion that made her heart skip a beat, but Seth's kiss had taken over her whole body, leaving her breathless.

Suddenly she heard Merlin's voice calling her name. Instantly calming her inner feelings and trying to act naturally, she walked towards his voice. He came into sight and stopped when he saw her. His whole face filled with a smile and Shasta realised that she loved him alone. What had happened with Seth she had to put behind her.

Running towards him, she explained that she had been for an early morning walk and, meeting Seth, she had commented on how lovely his garden looked. He had invited her for breakfast which she had accepted.

Merlin, walking back to her caravan with her, was becoming very moody as he heard this and it didn't go unnoticed by Shasta.

"Seth seems to have changed quite a bit lately and become a

much nicer person since the villagers have become friendlier towards him. Perhaps we should do the same, Merlin," she said.

Merlin did not agree but decided to hold his own counsel.

Chapter 35

Seth went back out to his garden to finish the patch he was working on and also to think about what had happened with Shasta.

Normally he was in control of his feelings; he usually took what he wanted from women and then left them. Being Jack the Lad with women was part of his reputation. He wasn't interested in what the villagers thought of him. They expected him to be drunk most of the time and take women on a whim, and he had lived up to their expectations. Since the first time that he had met Shasta, though, things had changed. Yes, he still had a few tankards of ale in the village tavern and entertained a woman now and again, but he was much quieter these days and the locals had remarked on it and become friendlier.

When he had kissed Shasta, it was as if someone else had taken over from him, producing an urgency he had not experienced before. Shasta had kissed him back with equal fervour, encouraging him and then drawing back and making excuses to leave. She and Merlin were betrothed, he knew that, but he didn't want to accept it and, if he could win her over, his life would be complete. This was the reason for the changes he had made; he hoped to let her see that he could change his habits.

When he had met her and May in the forest recently with their picnic, he had been making his way to the village, but had seen Shasta's caravan and decided to have a look round inside instead. This in itself was unusual for him. He respected other folk's privacy and property. As he had walked away from Shasta and May, he suddenly found himself outside of Shasta's caravan, yet he couldn't recall how he got there. Oh well, maybe it was something to do with the magic of the village.

He had been resting on his hoe as he had been passing these thoughts through his mind. Applying himself to the work in hand, he leant over once more and began to hoe between the flowers. Suddenly he felt there was someone behind him and yet he hadn't seen anyone approaching. As he stopped hoeing and turned round, he was startled to find a man he didn't recognise. As he got over his surprise, Seth noted that this man was dressed very expensively and was probably a good deal older than himself.

"I'm called Seth. Can I be of help to you, Sir?" he asked.

"I think it is I who can help you. Shall we go into the cottage?" the man replied.

Without waiting for an answer, Erasmus lifted the haggaday and walked in, expecting Seth to follow, which he did, silently.

Sitting in the chair at the table, Erasmus watched Seth for a few moments and said, "You must be wondering who I am and what I am doing here?" Without waiting for an answer he carried on. "My name is Erasmus. I have lived through many lifetimes and I am many hundreds of years old."

He allowed Seth to ponder on this before continuing, but Seth was far too confused to say anything anyway.

"You want the woman Shasta and, for personal reasons, I don't want Merlin to have her. Because of this, I am prepared to help you, but on my terms."

Seth was very wary of this man, Erasmus. He had suddenly appeared from nowhere, or so it seemed, and if he was to be believed he was hundreds of years old, which in itself made him want to smile with amusement.

He would have liked to win Shasta by fair means from Merlin and for her to come willingly, but could he trust this man? He doubted it.

Erasmus easily read his mind and he could see the glint in his eyes.

"You are a good looking young man, Seth, with a good strong body, and the women respond to that, as I saw earlier when you were with Shasta." Seeing his startled look he said. "You didn't see me, of course, because I wasn't here. I do not need to be here. I can be anywhere, even in a different country, but I can still see anything I choose to see. You felt that someone had taken over your body when you kissed Shasta. That was me, and if Shasta had opened her eyes she would have seen me leave your body. I wanted to know what it felt like to kiss a beautiful woman again after so many years. I can only do that if I enter a mortal's body. With Shasta it was particularly enjoyable. My time with her will not come for many years hence, after your lifetime of course, Seth."

This was only half true; Erasmus hoped to have her long before that, but he wasn't prepared to tell Seth that.

Seth hadn't moved from the moment that Erasmus had started talking. Not only had this person that outwardly looked like a man expressed an interest in the woman he wanted, he had entered his body to kiss her. At first he felt sick to the stomach, but then he suddenly realised that he still didn't know what Erasmus wanted of him.

Erasmus spoke again. "You want to know what I expect of you, Seth."

"Can you always read my mind?" Seth asked startled.

"Very easily. In fact you have been one of the easiest so far." Erasmus said. "It's very simple. If you want Shasta, you must get rid of Merlin. I will leave it up to you how you fulfil this task. For reasons I am not prepared to explain, he has to be got rid of by a mortal and that is the reason I cannot do it."

"I don't understand," said Seth. "If you are that powerful, why can't you do it and leave Shasta for me?" he asked as it seemed so simple to him.

For a moment Erasmus' face changed to a vile mask. His eyes turned into thin slits which became blood red and instantly changed back again so fast that Seth thought he had imagined it.

Erasmus, now calmer after being challenged, said, "Merlin and I have met before. I was unsuccessful then, so I intend to make sure this time."

With that, Erasmus stood up and, with a horrible cackle, he disappeared, leaving a thin trail of what looked like smoke.

Seth still hadn't moved and really began to wonder if he had imagined it all. But there was a sweet sickly smell in the cottage that had never been there before. It had arrived with Erasmus but stayed in the atmosphere. Standing up, Seth opened the door to let in some fresh air and tried to make some sense of it all. Was he losing his mind perhaps?

He had many things to think about if he wanted Shasta for himself. In the beginning he had been prepared to court her in the usual fashion, and bide his time, but now that had all changed.

He didn't want to kill Merlin; it wasn't in his nature to kill someone, let alone in cold blood.

He realised he had two choices. He could risk the wrath of Erasmus and try and court Shasta in the normal way to win her from Merlin. Or he could get rid of Merlin in a planned accident.

Somehow he didn't feel he should cross Erasmus, having seen his face turn to anger. At the same time he didn't want to hurt Merlin.

He went back outside to the garden to ponder on a satisfactory solution, the hoeing long forgotten.

He had seen Merlin drinking in the local tavern, although recently he had been spending more time with mistress Shasta. Perhaps it would be wise to try and offer his hand in friendship to him.

When Merlin left the fields with the other locals, they often walked past his cottage. He would suggest that they meet for a drink in the tavern in the village. If the other villagers saw that they were becoming friendly, suspicion hopefully wouldn't fall on his shoulders when anything untoward happened.

He was still unsure of his feelings about actually hurting Merlin. After all, Merlin had never done him any harm. In fact, on one occasion when he had been the worse for ale, Merlin had ensured that he got safely back to his cottage. Although he had not approved of his liaisons with the local married doxeys. Merlin's kindness had got the better of him. Seth had never got around to thanking him. Maybe this was the excuse he was looking for.

His mind made up, Seth waited for Merlin to return from the fields.

Unbeknown to Seth, Erasmus had been aware of his indecision over Merlin. The achievement of his goal was very close and he wasn't prepared to let anything go wrong, even if it meant eliminating Seth and using someone else.

He had tasted Shasta's mouth and he wanted much more, regardless of what it took to get it.

Chapter 36

Abelia sat on her lavender throne and sighed deeply. "I fear trouble ahead for Merlin."

This was said to none of the faeries in particular, but as Evening Primrose was closest she felt obliged to respond.

"What do you mean, your majesty?" she asked worriedly. All the faeries had a soft spot for him.

"I believe his life is in danger because of his betrothal to Shasta. She is a very beautiful woman and this wood cutter Seth is also showing an interest in her. Erasmus is also back and you know that he is an old adversary of mine. He will do anything to get rid of Merlin. His powers have got stronger recently and although he is immortal, he can also take on human form at will. His only weakness is his fondness for women. If he takes the life of a human, he will have to remain mortal for many years but without any powers. This has happened in the past because of Merlin, and he has only recently regained his powers. He is now ready for revenge. If we are to help Merlin, then we need May and Shasta's powers combined with mine. Now back to your duties and leave me to think."

Abelia reflected that her immortality had its' compensations but sometimes, just sometimes……. Oh well there was work to do.

Chapter 37

Shasta sat outside her caravan, still coming to terms with what had happened between her and Seth. She loved Merlin with her whole being. In fact she had travelled back into this lifetime, putting her own life at risk, to change history in an effort to save him. So why was Seth having this effect on her.

Over and over she had asked herself this question. It seemed that she had been unable to control her own actions. She couldn't deny that she had enjoyed kissing Seth, but it was only one kiss after all. She could never tell Merlin or May, but she felt a need to seek out May.

Walking through the gate of the cottage into the back garden, Shasta couldn't see May, yet she sensed that she was there. Following her instincts, she began to follow the path towards the end of the garden by the wishing well. Sure enough there was May by one of the fruit trees.

"Hello, May. the garden looks so beautiful I really enjoyed walking through and inhaling the lovely perfume of the many blooms," Shasta said.

"Thank you, mistress, It gives me great pleasure too."

"Tell me more about the wishing well, May," asked Shasta.

"The wishing well has always been in this garden and it enables me to visit Queen Abelia. Perhaps you would like to visit her yourself now that she has made her introduction to you, then you can see for yourself how it works?"

"She certainly looked beautiful in the vision I saw of her. Yes, I think I would like that. Could we go tonight, May, just the two of us?"

"Yes, of course, if you wish. My intuition tells me that Abelia is expecting us to visit anyway."

The decision having been made, May and Shasta made their way to the top of the garden to await Merlin's return from his work in the fields.

"I still don't see why I cannot come with you to see Abelia," said Merlin sulkily during their evening meal. "After all the faeries look forward to my company, I brighten up their evenings."

Shasta was amused by this and smiled lovingly at him. "It seems to me that most women are over-awed by your good looks," she said, knowing that he would be easily flattered. "I'm sorry, Merlin, but I need to do this without you. May is coming because I haven't visited Abelia before."

He still grumbled for a little while but said that he would go to the tavern for a glass or two of ale with Seth. Seeing Shasta's face change, and assuming that she was pleased that he was making an effort, Merlin stated that he had seen Seth on the way home earlier as he passed his cottage. They had talked for a while and Seth had made a point of thanking him for getting him home safely when he had been the worse for wear on a previous occasion.

* * *

As the night drew on, Merlin began his walk to the village, leaving Shasta and May to visit Abelia.

He was aware of soft footsteps behind him. Thinking he would enjoy company on the walk to the village, he turned expecting to see someone he knew but he was confronted by a stranger.

"Good evening, Sir. I don't think we have met before. My name is Merlin."

"Yes, I know," said the man quietly.

"I was walking to the local tavern for a glass of ale. Perhaps you would care to walk with me. Will you tell me your name?" Merlin asked as they fell into step together.

"My name is Erasmus," he said, trying not to show his hatred for Merlin.

"How do you know me? I don't think I have seen you in the village before?"

"I live on the far side, but I do hear the local gossip and I know that you are betrothed to Shasta. She is a very beautiful woman, Merlin. Ensure you don't lose her." Erasmus said.

"Have no fear of that. I have no intention of losing her," Merlin said with confidence.

On reaching the village Erasmus explained that he would be walking to his cottage on the far side of the green and declined Merlin's offer to buy him a tankard of ale.

He stood watching Erasmus for a while as he walked across the green, unable to make up his mind about him. There seemed to be an air of solitude about him. *Maybe he just likes to be alone*, thought Merlin. As this thought entered his head, Erasmus was suddenly no longer there although he had been in full view a few moments before. Merlin decided it was probably his eyes playing tricks as Erasmus was quite a distance off.

As he opened the door of the tavern, the combined smell of smoke, ale and sweat hit him all at once. Ribald laughter in one corner came from a local man with a young wench on his lap. She had her arms around his neck and was kissing him on the mouth, oblivious of the strong ale on his breath and the black rot of teeth. She was only interested in the few coins she would pick up by the end of the night, even if it meant being bedded for a few hours by men who had lost interest in their own wives. Slapping him heartily as he tried to kiss her again, she made her way towards Merlin. He didn't come into the tavern very often and several times she had tried to gain his interest.

As she approached him, she said, "How be, Merlin?"

Deep in thought, he automatically took a coin from his pocket and threw it on the bar without looking up. "You seem very distant, Merlin, my lovely. Can I make you feel better?" she asked as she put her hand on top of his leg suggestively.

"No thank you, Adie. I'm not in the mood for female company tonight," he said quietly.

Picking up the coin, she went to walk away to find a more accommodating customer.

"Do you know a man called Erasmus that lives on the other side of the village?" he asked.

"Nay, but I'll ask for you, my lovely," she said, eager to please him.

Leaving Merlin to his thoughts, she found another customer to keep her supplied with drink. He was the local smithy and sometimes wheelwright. When a cart was in need of general repair, the villagers would go to him because he favoured the barter system, unlike the other wheelwright who charged regular rates to suit his pocket.

Sitting comfortably on his ample knees, she allowed him to fondle her buxom bosom, precariously balanced just inside the top of her low cut blouse, before asking him, "Do 'ee know a man called Erasmus who lives on t'other side of the village?"

"Oh aye, he be a strange one, and they do say he casts bad spells and the like. You stay away from him, Adie. He be trouble and no mistake."

She agreed and stated that she was just asking for someone. Slapping away his hand which had been creeping down her cleavage as they spoke, she readjusted her breasts which were in danger of popping out over the top of her blouse, and made her way round the tavern earning her usual few coins here and there. Finally she reached Merlin in the hope of persuading him to spend time with her.

Placing her hand on the top of his thigh, this time with obvious intent, she told him what she had found out.

"Thank you, Adie," he said with a grin as he gently removed her hand from his thigh. "You're a beautiful, tempting, wench but I'm betrothed to Shasta and I would never hurt her."

"Can't blame a woman for trying, Merlin" she said with a coarse laugh and went back to earning her living.

Merlin saw a small unoccupied table in a far corner. Taking his drink over, he sat down and thought about this man called Erasmus. Judging by Adie's remarks, he didn't seem very popular in the village.

He had often watched May cast spells, but she only ever did them for the good of the village. No spells were ever cast to hurt anyone. If Erasmus lived on the far side of the village, this could be the reason Merlin had not made his acquaintance. Yet his instinct convinced him that they had met before somewhere. While he pondered on this, the door of the tavern opened, distracting his thoughts. Adie was going outside with one of the field hands he knew well. They were so preoccupied with one another they bumped into Seth who was just coming in the door at the same time. Merlin, although still having slight reservations which he had kept to himself, bought Seth a drink and they took it over to the table he was occupying. Merlin watched Seth silently as he acknowledged most of the occupants of the tavern. Generally they seemed a lot friendlier towards him these days and it seemed to make him more amiable. He also reluctantly acknowledged that Seth was a good looking man and he could understand why all the women were attracted to him, including Shasta, if he was honest with himself.

As Seth raised his tankard to drink Merlin asked, "Have you met a man called Erasmus, Seth? Apparently he lives over the other side of the village."

Choking on his ale, and with a face drained of colour, Seth tried to recover his composure, but to no avail. As Merlin asked him if he was alright, Seth explained it away by stating that his drink had gone down the wrong way.

"Why do you ask, Merlin?" he said, still trying to regain his composure.

"I met him on the way to the village and he said he knew me. I assumed it was because I am betrothed to Shasta which everyone knows about. He also said that she was a beautiful woman and to ensure I didn't lose her. I have no intention of doing that. I just wondered if you had come across him when you came to the village at any time," Merlin replied.

"I only have a nodding acquaintance with him, Merlin," Seth said guardedly, but also beginning to relax again slightly.

Merlin decided to forget about Erasmus for a while and joined in with the general ambience of the tavern. Now and again he took a girl on his knee and gave her a chaste kiss and sent her on her way. Sometimes, if he felt generous, he included a coin here and there. Seth also joined in, never at a loss for women, and his popularity stronger than before. He was also ensuring that he drank in moderation these days. With his intention to marry foremost in his thoughts, he needed to show some responsibility. Merlin began to wonder how Shasta was fairing with Abelia and decided to leave the tavern early. Seth, finishing his ale, said that he would leave also and they could walk back together. As they walked, laughing at stories they had heard during the evening. Seth started to feel rather unusual. His head began to buzz and it felt as if it had a steel band being tightened around it, compressing the sides, which could not be put down to an excess of drink as he had only had two tankards of ale. Merlin, noticing that Seth had suddenly gone quiet and that he was holding his hand to his head, asked him if he was alright.

As Seth took his hand away from his head, Merlin watched in horror as his face suddenly became contorted as if in pain and seemed to change shape into a face that Merlin recognised and never expected to ever see again. Rooted to the spot, he failed to notice that Seth had now got his right hand behind his back. Reaching for the dagger that he always carried sheathed on his belt, Seth raised his arm, the dagger in his hand, ready to plunge it downwards into Merlin. As Merlin tried to back away, he tripped and fell. The last thing he remembered was hearing Seth shouting NO, Nooooo… as he fought to stop the knife plunging into Merlin.

Chapter 38

Shasta and May had walked to the bottom of the garden by the wishing well as Merlin had been making his way to the village. Shasta marvelled at the unique way she and May had arrived at Faery Cove; the process of drinking from the well, the sudden reduction in height and the magnificence of the faeries and their clothes was something she could only experience first hand.

Queen Abelia had been awaiting their arrival and was seated on her throne, talking to Princess Day Lily while they waited.

"Your majesty seems preoccupied and sad," Day Lily observed in her gentle way.

"Many things are happening, Day Lily. Erasmus has been quiet for some years now, and it seemed almost too good to be true, but since Shasta came to the village, he has been up to serious mischief. We will all have to watch him more closely. Hush now, my dear, our visitors are here …. Hello, May, and welcome to my kingdom, Shasta."

"I'm very pleased to meet you, your majesty" Shasta said.

"Oh please call me Abelia. You and I will be friends for many meetings to come, both now and in the future," she said. "There are many things we have to talk about, Shasta, as there is evil in the making. First, though, we will have refreshments. Faeries, please bring our guests a drink."

* * *

Sipping their drink from tiny acorn cups, May, Shasta and Abelia were now sitting in her toadstool house.

"Shasta, because I know everything that happens in the village, I am aware of what took place between you and Seth the woodcutter."

For a moment Shasta looked startled at Abelia's forthrightness. If truth be told she was also a little embarrassed.

"Don't be embarrassed, Shasta. I know everything that happens. It wasn't Seth who instigated the kiss, but Erasmus."

Whilst Shasta looked confused by this, May, who had been sitting quietly until now, tried to hide her emotions. She had known the kiss would happen, of course, but didn't know when. She just hoped that Shasta would confide in her when it did. It was Merlin that she felt sorry for. He would be devastated. Easily reading May's mind, Abelia said, "Don't prejudge, May, until you have heard all the facts."

Abelia began to explain about Erasmus and her past connections with him, how on several occasions they had confronted one another. Erasmus loved manipulating people's minds and planting ideas, thoughts and suggestions to suit his own evil ends. Mostly Abelia had managed to get the upper hand with him - at least as far as she knew, she had.

"Forgive my ignorance, Abelia, but how do you mean you confronted one another?" Shasta asked.

"Let me try to explain. Sometimes Erasmus comes to me as a vision. It's his way of letting me know that he has been up to no good. On one occasion he cast a spell over my kingdom which stopped me seeing what was happening in the village. Fortunately, a couple of the villagers were walking past his cottage. Normally the animal skins covering the windows to keep out the draught prevent anyone from looking in, but on this occasion they were pulled back. Out of curiosity they looked in and saw him with his back to them, hunched over a cauldron, mumbling. Seeing a vision of Merlin rise out of the cauldron, they waited to see what would happen next. Erasmus was not aware of them at first but, sensing they were there, he turned and his face contorted into a grotesque mask. The men ran off in fear of their lives, frightened to tell anyone at first in case of reprisals by Erasmus, but then their tongues became loose over a tankard of ale in the tavern."

Seeing Shasta's startled face, Abelia instantly reassured her that all was well. "He has been rather quiet of late, though, which does concern me, I must admit. So you see, my dear, he can be very dangerous. Although I am used to his games, he is quite capable of entering anyone's mind and, if there is any weakness, he will play on it and manipulate them."

"He sounds a thoroughly despicable person," said Shasta with a shudder. "I hope I never come into contact with him again, either mentally or visibly."

"You won't, Shasta. I will protect you!" Abelia vowed.

As Abelia uttered the words, she suddenly felt a very strong icy feeling around her, indicating danger, which made her shudder. She tried to see beyond the kingdom but it was hazy. Concerned by this, Abelia knew that there was only one person responsible. Surely it wasn't possible. The change in Abelia didn't go unnoticed by May who had remained quiet during this exchange. She had only seen her react once before in this manner, when there had been a murder in the village. That was many years ago, though. Shasta, preoccupied by all that had been said, was completely unaware until May said, "Are you alright, Abelia. Is there something wrong?"

"I share your apprehension, May," Shasta said, her stomach suddenly niggling with worry, but why should that be so, she wondered.

"I fear there is, May. I'm having difficulty seeing beyond the kingdom and, as we discussed, there is probably only one person responsible," she said, very concerned.

"Maybe Shasta and I should leave the kingdom, Abelia, and see what we can find out," May said.

"That would be very helpful, May," she said.

Instantly May and Shasta were back by the wishing well at normal height.

"Come," May said to Shasta, "I know it's late but let's go to the village and see if we can find out what is happening."

As Shasta started to walk towards the top of the garden, May did something she hadn't done for years and had promised herself she wouldn't do again - she mentally transported them to the edge of the village green. It was worth it to see Shasta face. After explaining how she did it, she and Shasta started to look around to see if anyone was about. Instantly they felt tension in the air. The obvious answer was to look in the tavern which would still be open. As May opened the door, followed by Shasta, they were greeted by a deathly silence.

"What's happened?" Shasta asked the nearest man.

"Oh, mistress, Merlin has been stabbed and he may not survive," the man said.

Shasta felt a searing pain in her stomach and clutched it in agony as she passed out. Fortunately, the man was able to stop her falling too heavily by breaking her fall.

May stood rooted to the spot, unable to take any of it in. Gathering her wits, she made herself move towards Shasta. Kneeling on the straw on the floor she cradled Shasta's head in her arms. Groaning, Shasta started to come around. "Please tell me it isn't true, May," she asked as she tried to rise.

May looked at the long faces of the villagers which confirmed it.

"Who did it?" asked Shasta in earnest.

"It be Seth," said one.

"No, it be someone who looked like Seth but his face was different," said another who had seen what had happened. "Seth held the dagger in his hand but the devil himself had taken over, and Seth tried to stop it happening."

"Where is Merlin? I must go to him," Shasta said, trying to regain her senses as best she could.

"He be at the cottage of Adie on the edge of the green," said a couple of voices almost in unison.

"I will come with you, mistress," May said.

Both women left the tavern and made their way to the cottage with a couple of the other villagers tagging along and showing them the way.

Shasta, without waiting to knock, burst through the door, much to the surprise of Adie who was kneeling on the floor beside her pallet on which Merlin had been laid. She was just replacing a wet cloth over his brow.

"Oh, mistress Shasta, I fear the worst. Who would do this to him?" she asked, her face showing the signs of many tears. "The doctor is coming but he maybe some time yet as he's delivering a child."

Shasta, not listening, rushed over to Merlin and knelt beside Adie whilst noting the dark congealed blood which had stained Merlin's doublet. His face was ashen. Adie reluctantly exchanged places with Shasta who took Merlin's cold hand in hers and placed it against her face. Through her tears, she sobbed, "My beloved Merlin, I can't live without you. Please don't leave me. I came back to save you from death. God forbid that I have failed you. Why didn't I take you with me tonight and maybe this wouldn't have happened. Perhaps I can't change history after all. Oh, Merlin, my love, please open your eyes."

May, Adie and the two men who had accompanied them moved towards the door to give Shasta privacy. They stood not knowing what to say or do. May was equally devastated but it was Shasta's place to be beside Merlin now.

The door opened and a flustered doctor arrived, carrying a tatty looking bag.

"Well, one fine boy delivered into the world and, by the looks of this, one fine young man about to depart it," he said in a matter of fact voice as he glanced at Merlin.

Shasta, on hearing this, let out a strangled sob. "Please try to save him. You are his last hope," she said.

"Then leave me be to get on with my work and stand with the others by the door," The doctor replied brusquely.

As Shasta stood up and turned, May put out her arms to enfold her as she would a young child.

"Oh, May, I'm so frightened of losing him. I came back to this life to try and save him, and I have failed."

"Hush, child, his life is in the hands of fate."

The doctor opened Merlin's shirt to get a better look at the wound and, in doing so, caused the wound to bleed afresh. At this, Merlin groaned as a renewed wave of pain hit him.

"I saw some Fuga Daemonum growing outside. Woman, will you please go and pick a handful or more for me?" the doctor said, looking kindly at May.

May and the doctor had discovered many new cures through trial and error and they had a mutual respect for one another.

"Come, Shasta, will you help me? It will keep our minds occupied," she said gently.

Glancing firstly at Merlin, she agreed, still terrified that something would happen if she left the room. Adie also went out with them and, being a bit naïve about herbs, asked May why he would want this Fuga whatever-it-was-called.

"Because," said May patiently as they all began to gather the flowers, "it has magical and medicinal properties. Normally it's harvested on St. Johns Day - June 24th - that is why it has the common name of St. Johns Grass. It's also known as John's Wort or Goat Weed. Adie, surely you must have seen it hung over doors. It is renowned for warding off evil spirits."

"Oh, aye, you mean those shrivelled up flowers that look as if they're dead, May? My friend has some hanging. I wondered what they were for."

After they had gathered a large bunch each, May took hold of all of them and led the way back into the cottage. Shasta once more hovered uncertainly near the pallet.

If anything Merlin looked worse than before.

"Give me some light, woman" the doctor said, irrespective of the reverence normally paid to her. Then, in a more kindly voice, he added, "Stand by his head, if you wish."

She hurried to his head and fell on her knees so she could touch his face easily. May began mashing some of the flowers to produce the required amount of oil. Having prepared what she considered to be enough, she took the mortar over to the doctor. Heedless of hygiene, and having already bared Merlin's chest, he began to gently massage the oil into the wound. At this, Merlin groaned at the extra pain inflicted on him, little realising that it would help heal the wound. When this was done, May helped the doctor cover the wound. Adie, in the meantime, under May's instruction had made an infusion by steeping the flowers in boiling water. This would act as a painkiller and quench his thirst. Having strained the liquid, which had now cooled, into a cup, she gave it to May. Instructing Shasta to gently lift his head, she put the cup to Merlin's lips to enable him to sip the drink. More was spilt on the cloth under the cup than actually drunk, but it at least moistened his lips.

The doctor stood up and rubbed his knees which had now begun to cramp. A man of few words, he said, "Only time will tell now. I will come back if needs be, May. You know where to find me."

With that he was gone.

Realising that they could do nothing else, the two villagers hovering by the door also took their leave, although May and Shasta were unaware of them going. Adie, deciding that she would probably be in the way, decided to join them and return to the cottage later. If there was anyone left in the tavern she could tell her story and be the centre of attention for once.

During the night Merlin seemed to improve for a while, giving Shasta hope, but then he deteriorated, fast falling in and out of consciousness. As the cock crowed at dawn, Merlin let out one long shuddering sigh, and with Shasta's name on his lips, he died. Shasta's screams of anguish could be heard resounding around the village. May rocked her in her arms as she would a baby, but she was inconsolable. Pulling free, Shasta ran from the cottage, blindly bumping into villagers and anything that got in her way. Finally reaching her caravan, soaked in sweat from her exertions, she flung herself down on the bed. "Oh, Merlin," she sobbed through her tears, "I can't bear to live without you."

Instantly her mind was made up. Running into the forest, she wildly pulled up as many fungi and plants as she knew to be poisonous, and started to eat them. She was then violently sick and passed out.

* * *

Shasta was aware that she was lying on a pallet of straw with someone's breath very close to her face. At first, she was reluctant to open her eyes as she knew that her attempts to take her life had failed. Eventually she opened her eyes to see Seth staring down at her. She was in his cottage. Merlin was dead and this man was responsible if the villagers were to be believed. She screamed in horror and tried to raise herself but was too weak to move.

"Please, mistress, hear me before you judge me," he said.

Unable to move, Shasta had no choice. "How did I get here?" she asked him.

"I be hiding from the villagers. They wanted to hang me from the oak. I swear, mistress, it weren't me that killed Merlin," he said, his accent returning with his fear.

Shasta asked him again how she got to his cottage. Seth told her how he and Merlin had spent an enjoyable evening supping ale and then, on the way back, he suddenly seemed to have no control over his actions. He had tried to stop himself from stabbing Merlin. He explained that it was as if someone had taken control of his body and he suspected it was Erasmus. He hesitated before he said the name, almost afraid of letting the word leave his lips. He also told her of all his recent experiences with Erasmus and how he had suddenly turned up at the cottage.

"I hid in the middle of the forest, mistress, and I heard this terrible squawking noise. I got curious and followed the sound. I saw you lying on the ground with a magpie standing beside you squawking for all its worth. I usually see them in pairs, so I knew it meant trouble. There was dirt round your mouth and when I looked inside there were bits of fungus and mistletoe. So I cleared it all out with my fingers and when I lifted you up to carry you back here you were sick again all over me. I saw what happened at Adie's cottage with the plants you picked 'n' all, and I made you an infusion with foxgloves to clear out everything. Most folk think I don't know anything, but my family always used herbs. You've been here two days now. I think everything you are going to get rid of must be gone by now, and your brow is no longer fevered. I haven't left your side, mistress."

This all came out in one breath. To Shasta it sounded as if he had been trying to make amends for everything that had occurred, including getting her better when that was the last thing she had wanted to happen. Now she looked properly at Seth, she noticed the black rings under his eyes, probably from lack of sleep and worrying in case he was found by the villagers. He had also taken a chance bringing her back to his cottage to look after her. That surely would have been the first place they would have looked for him. Maybe, just maybe, he was telling the truth about what happened to Merlin. He had also saved her life, even though she was trying to kill herself. Maybe she wasn't meant to die and fate intended her to live. What would life hold for her without Merlin, though? He had become her whole life and that was why she had come back to save him.

As all these thoughts passed through her mind, she suddenly felt very weak and tired and unable to think clearly any more. Seth was making her another infusion and, as she watched him, she felt a great wave of pain rush through her which made her cry out again in anguish. Instantly he was at her side.

"What ails thee, mistress. is there anything I can do?"
Shaking her head she turned her back to him and sobbed silently
for her lost love.

Chapter 39

"I can't find her anywhere, Abelia," May said, having taken comfort in Faery Cove. She couldn't believe that Merlin was gone, and whilst she had been relating all that had happened in the village, Abelia had allowed the faeries to sit with them and listen. She had been unable to see anything outside her kingdom, therefore Erasmus had been up to his tricks. Even so, he still hadn't appeared to her in order to gloat, as he had done in the past.

What was he up to?

The faeries sat around in stunned silence. Some were crying quietly. They were all very fond of Merlin and his jocular ways, and now they would never see him again. Why hadn't Abelia shown her feelings some, wondered. She had sat in silence, her face unchanged, since May had first told them.

Abelia, of course, would grieve in the privacy of her toadstool later on when it was quiet. There were many things to do and, first, Shasta had to be found. Curse Erasmus for the spell he had put over her. She was still unable to see outside the kingdom and had to rely on May for information. With Shasta here, the three of them could work on breaking the spell together. Three heads were better than one any day.

Fate predicted that she would take her own life to be joined again with Merlin, but Abelia's instinct told her that she was still alive and somewhere near the forest.

She voiced her opinion to May who suddenly put her hand to her mouth. Of course that was where she would be found. Why hadn't she gone to the far edge of the woods? As this thought occurred to her, she suddenly thought of something else; Seth lived in a cottage on the other side of the forest. Could Shasta possibly be there? He made no secret of the fact that he wanted her, if the gossips were to be believed. Unintentionally reading May's mind, Abelia agreed with her line of thought.

"I must get back to the village," May said, her mind made up as to what to do. "I will return when I have news, Abelia," and, with that, she was gone.

In her haste she had once again forgotten her promise to herself and transported herself directly to the village, much to the surprise of some of the locals standing around talking over recent events. This was to her advantage, though. May explained that she needed their help in searching for Shasta. Yes, she knew that they had already looked for her, but this time they needed to go deeper into the forest as she felt that maybe Seth had something to do with her disappearance. This was the incentive she knew that they needed, as they perhaps would not only find the mistress but Seth into the bargain.

Spreading out to search, and calling out to others on the way, it wasn't long before most of the villagers had joined in. This hadn't really been May's intention but there was safety in numbers, she thought. They covered the forest from beginning to end and eventually, by nightfall, had reached the outer edge leading to Seth's cottage. Instinct told May that she was there and, instructing the crowd to wait where they were, she walked up the path to the door, noting the neat and orderly flowers with not a weed to be seen. Even the front of the cottage looked well-maintained. This was not what she had heard in the past, only that it was all run down and the garden was weed-infested. So what had brought about the change, she wondered. With some trepidation she knocked on the door.

It was some time before it was opened by Seth looking very haggard and drawn.

"I have been expecting you, May, and as you can see she is here. I have been looking after her."

Very briefly he filled her in on what had happened and invited her in, noting with some concern the crowd at the end of his path.

May wasted no time in going to her mistress, seeing that she was very pale and thin. Shasta tried to raise her head and May supported it with her arm. She told May what had happened to her and that Seth had saved her life.

"So I understand, mistress, but let's not forget that he also killed Merlin."

Seeing the distress and sudden tears in Shasta's eyes, she instantly regretted having said it. "I'm sorry to have upset you, mistress. I miss him too."

"Seth has explained to me what happened, May, and I believe him," Shasta said. "Seth, please tell May what happened."

So, once again, Seth told the story of how he had tried to stop it happening. May, thinking back to what the locals had said in the tavern about it being Seth but his face was different, reluctantly began to believe him. She didn't want to, because she didn't particularly like him, but it did make sense, she supposed.

"It seems I may have misjudged you, Seth, but that doesn't mean I like you. I thank you, though, for saving the mistress' life."

"I admit I wanted mistress Shasta for myself and would have done anything to make her my wife, but I would never kill anyone in cold blood. Erasmus somehow forced my hand. It was as if he was in my head and I couldn't get rid of him. He be evil that man, if he be a man that is."

No sooner than the words had left his mouth, Seth suddenly grabbed his head, rocking it back and forth, screaming with pain. May shrunk back towards Shasta in fear as his face contorted and changed into Erasmus. Oblivious of the women, Erasmus spoke through Seth.

"You are a weakling and a coward, you lowly worm. I had to force you to put the dagger in Merlin. I have taken a human life and therefore have to pay the consequences for all eternity because of you."

The words boomed out of his mouth and, in a final act of

revenge, he inflicted even more pain on Seth. Holding his head and unable to take any more, Seth fell to the floor screaming, his face changing back to his own as he did so. The door flew open as the villagers all tried to get in at once to see what was happening. They had heard Erasmus from outside. The nearest man checked Seth for any signs of breathing and declared that he was obviously dead.

"Mayhap we misjudged him after all," said one and the others agreed in unison, including May.

Two men had died because of her, thought Shasta, and both of them in love with her. She tried to feel some emotion for Seth but just felt sadness in the way that he had died. Merlin had been her only love. She still felt shock at seeing Erasmus' face, it was pure evil and she didn't want to see it again. To think that he had kissed her mouth, albeit through Seth. She rubbed at her mouth viciously and shuddered. Fortunately no-one noticed.

"Looks like we have another body to bury, then," said one of the men to no-one in particular. Someone found some sheeting and gently wrapped Seth's body in it. They loaded it onto his cart, which was nearby, and two men began to pull it back through the forest to the village. On reaching the village, they were aware of a fire in the distance. One of the men asked a spectator where the fire was.

"It be that weird 'uns place at the far end of the village green. No one knows how it started, though. Let it burn to the ground, I say," he said vehemently.

* * *

"Oh, May, I tried so hard to make things right and I got everything wrong," Shasta said now that they were alone.

"Hush, child, no-one could change what has happened here. It was meant to be. Now we must get you better. If we bring the cart back, do you think you could travel on it back to my cottage? We can't leave you here."

"I think so, May," she said quietly.

Having made the arrangements, May went back to sit with Shasta. For something to do she began to reheat the infusion that Seth had made to give to Shasta. Although she couldn't eat anything, her mistress could at least have a warm drink inside her. Once back in the village she could look after her properly with her own potions and herbs, although she had to admit that Seth had done a good job. She silently admitted to herself that she had quite probably misjudged him in many ways. For that she felt some guilt.

Once again propping up Shasta's head, she helped her to sip the drink. Slowly the colour began to come back to her face.

Shasta was transferred back to May's cottage and she took over Merlin's bed from which she took some comfort. Slowly her health began to improve. May had been to see Abelia and reported all that had happened, including the fire at Erasmus' cottage, although there was no sign of him anywhere. Once Shasta was back to her full strength they would both visit Abelia and decide what to do about Erasmus. By his own admission, albeit through Seth, he had been instrumental in killing a mortal and for that he would pay the consequences.

Shasta's health improved thanks to May's expertise, although she still held an air of desolation about her. No-one ever expected her to get over the death of Merlin - that became obvious on talking to her.

Sitting in May's garden one evening a couple of weeks later, they decided to visit Abelia.

Going down to the wishing well they went through the usual procedure to meet Evening Primrose who guided her along with the other faeries to Abelia.

"Welcome, Shasta. It's good to see you are recovered," Abelia said.

"Thank you, Abelia, I do feel better, although I wish I had succeeded in joining Merlin. I miss him so much," She said with unashamed tears starting to fall again.

"Day Lily, will you get Shasta a drink from my toadstool, please."

For a moment Day Lily was taken aback; no faeries were usually allowed in Abelia's toadstool for any reason.

"Which drink would you like me to get, your majesty?" she asked.

"The blue container in the first cupboard has a transparent phial in it. Please pour the liquid into a cup and bring it to me," She said patiently.

"Very well, your majesty."

Returning with the drink she gave it to Abelia.

Abelia gave it to Shasta and told her to sip it slowly. As Shasta did so, she saw visions of Merlin appear. He seemed to be sitting quite alone with his elbow resting on his knee and his face leaning on his fist.

"Oh, Merlin," she said, tears welling up in her eyes.

He looked up at this and smiled at her. She desperately wanted to touch him and hold him once again, but somehow she knew this was impossible. He was dressed in the blue doublet she had first seen him in after he had transformed from a cat. She remembered how handsome she had thought him then. That was when she had made her decision to come back to this life to ensure that he would always remain human.

"Oh, Merlin" she said again. "It all went so wrong for us."

His face seemed to tell her differently. He was still smiling as the vision faded. Shasta had the feeling that she would see him again, but how that was possible she had no idea. She looked at Abelia and thanked her.

"Trust me, Shasta, you will meet again. You were destined to be together for all time. First we have to deal with Erasmus. I know he is still in the village but his power is getting weaker because the haze has lifted from our kingdom and I can see outside again. I intend to summon him here in a vision but I need help from both of you. We will go to my toadstool, I think, and then the other faeries will not be frightened unnecessarily."

Having settled themselves, May and Shasta sat facing Abelia. With combined concentration they called on Erasmus to appear.

Nothing happened.

"Erasmus, I call on you to face the consequences of your actions. Accept that we are stronger than you and appear now." Almost at once, they began to notice a sweet sickly smell and Erasmus appeared in front of them.

From Shasta there was a sharp intake of breath.

"Fear not, my dear. he cannot hurt us. He is resigned to his fate."

Although she relaxed a bit, Shasta was still wary and moved a bit closer to May for reassurance.

"Erasmus, you were determined for Merlin to be slain by a human hand to exonerate you from blame. When Seth fought against it, you entered his body in anger and took over. In effect, therefore, you killed Merlin yourself. This is the second time in five hundred years that you have had to be punished. You also know that you will lose your powers until we consider that you have served your punishment. Therefore, as this is the second time, I have cast the following spell, which you will be unable to revoke. From this day forth you will become a book known as 'The Eye of Erasmus' and May will be the keeper. No longer will you have any incentive to be evil and will only wish to do good deeds."

"I agree to everything you say, Abelia, if you will grant me the power of speech".

Abelia thought about this and said, "Very well, Erasmus, I will grant you speech but at Mays' discretion only. If she wishes to talk to you, then you may answer her. The book, to be known as 'The Eye of Erasmus', will be as follows. The querent will approach the book with a question. You will then allow the book to fall open on a rhyme which the querent will read. This will give them the understanding on how to achieve the answer. You will ensure that the rhyme is easy to understand. At no time will you try and confuse them, and you will never let the book tell a lie. This I charge you with."

"Very well, Abelia, I agree."

"You have no choice, Erasmus," and with that the vision disappeared and a very large dusty book appeared in front of May. Both Shasta and May jumped in surprise and, as May put out her hand towards the book, an eye opened lazily and then closed again.

"So, Erasmus, it appears that I am in charge of you. Take heed of all that Abelia has said and all will be well."

May picked up the book, which was lighter than she expected, and placed it in front of herself again. Satisfied with what had taken place, Abelia said, "You will be the keeper of the book for many years to come, May. Use it to your advantage. Erasmus has accepted his fate and he will be no further trouble, I promise you."

"Very well, Abelia. Now let's go back to the cottage, Shasta," May said, retrieving the book as she stood up.

Shasta was unsure of her feelings now. It was lovely to see the vision of Merlin and know that some day they would meet again. Pondering on this thought, she followed May to the familiar back door of the cottage.

May, on entering, went straight to where she kept her herbs and placed the book on the shelf. As she turned her back, Erasmus once again lazily opened his eye and looked around.

"Oh well", he thought, "it could have been worse, May was an attractive woman and he could always watch her unobtrusively, and Shasta would be his eventually. His work here was finished now, but he could wait indefinitely if need be. He had tasted her mouth and she was worth waiting for."

Smiling he closed his eye again. He would be a book for at least two hundred years, so he may as well get used to it.

I just hope May keeps me dusted, he thought as he dozed off again.

Chapter 40

The present

"Erasmus hasn't been to visit you lately, May. Is everything alright?" Iris asked.

They had been stocking up on food in the village and were now enjoying a cooling drink. George had opted to stay at the cottage. He had been lazing in the garden and was reluctant to move.

"It does seem strange that he hasn't been around," said May, hiding her disappointment from her sister. "Perhaps he's been busy," she said, making excuses on his behalf.

Having finished their drink they made there way back to the cottage with the shopping, sharing it evenly between them. They took a slow walk which didn't take them very long. On days that they did the shopping, they had fallen into the pattern of cooking their evening meal by magic. It was not only quicker but it was worth it for May to watch Iris' face which still appeared childlike whenever she witnessed it. Iris would find life very hard when she returned to her own home.

As they neared the cottage May noticed a small, thin, black cat sitting by the gate.

"Surely not" she thought…….. "It can't be………… Oh no………."

Dropping the shopping bags much to the surprise of Iris, she rushed forward, ready to scoop him up in her arms, having no doubt in her mind that it was Merlin. As she got closer the cat stood up and began to walk towards her, meowing piteously. She scooped him up and out of earshot said, "Merlin is it really you? Are you all right? You look so thin?"

She was desperate for news of Shasta but reluctant to worry her sister too much.

"Yes, but who's that?" he asked whilst they were still out of Iris' hearing.

"That's my sister, Iris. She and her husband are staying with me. Tell me everything tonight when they have gone to bed. In the meanwhile, you are a normal cat who has been lost and returned."

Iris had picked up the extra bags and was struggling to catch up with May.

"Whose cat is that, May, and why all the fuss?"

"This is Snoops, Iris. I thought I had lost him. He wandered off a long time ago. I'm so happy to have him back; he's company for me. To celebrate him coming back he can have a big, fat, juicy piece of fish tonight for his tea. He needs fattening up again by the look of things."

May walked up her path to the front door whilst Merlin rubbed against her legs, almost tripping her. She couldn't wait to hear what had happened, but was concerned to see that Merlin had returned to being a cat. Oh well, she would just have to be patient and wait until later tonight when they had gone to bed. She didn't dare take the chance yet of letting her sister and George hear Merlin talking. They would realise straightaway who he was and she wanted to prepare Iris slowly. Having finished their evening meal, George and May settled down for the evening in the cosy chintz settee, whilst May favoured her rocking chair as usual, but this evening she had Merlin on her lap. He had eaten his fish and was settled purring happily as May stroked the back of his coat. *He feels so thin*, she thought to herself, *I can almost feel his ribs. My poor Merlin what has happened to you and where can mistress Shasta be I wonder? Well not long to wait now before I find out*, she thought.

George sat reading the paper whilst Iris and May discussed the following morning's work which would be to continue making up potions for the villagers. Iris had really got the hang of it and sometimes May left her to experiment on her own.

Eventually, and much to May's delight, Iris suggested they went to bed. George, agreeing, pulled Iris playfully from the settee. With his arm round her waist, they said goodnight to May and retired, closing the bedroom door behind them. May indicated for Merlin to be quiet for a while until she was sure that they were asleep.

"Please, Merlin, tell me all that has happened, and what news of Shasta?" May asked.

"Oh May it was so wonderful to lead a normal life as a human again." Then slowly he began to relate all that had happened up until his death. To suddenly become a cat again, though, was as upsetting to him as it was to May.

"I feel doomed to stay being a cat whether I like it or not, and I miss Shasta so much, May," he said, feeling very sorry for himself.

"Well at least you're still alive, Merlin, even if you are a cat. We'll have to ensure that Iris and George don't realise that you can speak for the time being, I think it will cause complications. So just remember that when they are around. In the meantime I am just pleased that you are back with me."

That evening, after May had retired to bed, Merlin lay curled up in his favourite chair in the kitchen revelling in the warmth and comfort. He thought about all that had happened from the time that he and Shasta had left this lifetime. He was not aware of leaving Shasta during this transition, only that he was suddenly living with May in his previous lifetime, and then finally of his death at the hands of Erasmus. Oh yes, it was him. At first he was shocked and startled to see Seth's face change into Erasmus', but he was instantly recognisable. He had been so shocked that he had been unable to defend himself. It was strange also that he couldn't remember the exact time that he had turned back into a cat again, only that he had suddenly arrived back at May's cottage. The last thing he remembered was seeing Shasta in a vision and knowing in his heart that they would meet again.

As he began to fall asleep, he wondered when that would finally be and would he remain a cat indefinitely?

So the past cannot be changed then, thought May, as she lay in bed going over all that Merlin had told her. What of this other Erasmus, though, that Merlin had spoken of, she wondered. Surely it couldn't be *her* Erasmus, could it? Yes, she admitted to herself, that was how she now thought of him. Her feelings were getting stronger for him and she was sure that he felt the same. However, she hadn't seen him for a couple of weeks, which was unusual. In fact she had made discreet enquiries in the village and no-one had seen him. Slowly she drifted into a fitful sleep, her imagination conjuring up unusual dreams about her imagined past life. Perhaps she was better off living in the present after all.

Chapter 41

The past

As Shasta sat talking to May one evening, she realised that she had been putting off her return to her own time. She had failed in what she had tried to do and had to accept that, but she still found it difficult to leave.

"Perhaps you should ask the question of Erasmus," said May.

So far she had been reluctant to ask him anything. Lifting the book from the shelf, Shasta set it down between them on the table. As Abelia had instructed, she thought about the question she needed an answer to, and waited while Erasmus came up with the expected rhyme.

The only words on the page were:

He waits for you, in pastures new.

"I wonder what that means," she asked May, at the same time trying not to get too excited.

"Perhaps he is waiting for you in your own time, mistress. I will miss your company but I feel the time has come for you to return."

"Oh, May, I will miss you so much, even though you will be alive in my time."

"Can you tell me what I'm like, mistress? Do I look any different? There are so many questions that I have wanted to ask you."

"You dress very similarly to what you are wearing now and you still make up potions for the villagers. In fact nothing about Shasta in my time is very different. Shasta Day is still celebrated on the green and we dress up in the clothes of today. In fact you meet a man during the celebrations and fall in love. I won't know what happens until I get back, but I believe you will marry."

"What's his name" May asked full of curiosity.

"Erasmus."

May's hand had been resting lightly on the book until she heard this. Hastily she withdrew it as if she had been burnt.

"Surely not, mistress. You must be mistaken."

"No, there is no mistake I assure you, May. In my lifetime he is a very pleasant man. Perhaps his time spent as a book has mellowed him and maybe, just maybe, he has learnt his lesson. I think I will spend one last night with you and then I must go."

The following morning Shasta went to the field to collect her horse. Recognising his mistress, he galloped towards her. Giving him a rub on his nose, she took hold of his reins and walked him back to the caravan which she had prepared ready for travelling. The hardest part was saying goodbye to May and eventually she suggested that she rode beside her into the village where she would say a final farewell to her and the other villagers.

As she approached the village green, she was startled to see that the whole of the village had turned up to say goodbye. Part of her was tempted to stay but realistically she knew that she had to leave. Saying a final goodbye to May she headed the horse out of the village and onto the road she had originally come in by. As the horse trotted slowly through the country lanes, Shasta noticed how much brighter everything seemed to be. The strength of the sun on her face made her feel very sleepy and taking an old wide-brimmed hat she placed it on her head so that it shaded her eyes. Listening to the birds as they sang sweetly, she began to close her eyes, knowing that her horse would be her guide.

How she would get back to her own time would be entirely left to chance.

Chapter 42

Shasta was aware of laughter in the distance. Unsure at first whether she was dreaming or not, she kept her eyes closed and just listened. Eventually curiosity got the better of her and, opening her eyes, she could only see blue sky with a few puffballs of cloud here and there. Realising that she must have been asleep she was at first startled.

She raised her head slightly from the hayrick she appeared to be resting against and looked around her. In the distance the men were haymaking whilst smaller children were throwing handfuls of chaff over each other and rolling in any that fell to the ground.

Raising her arms and stretching, she wondered how she came to be there.

She stood up, brushed off the bits of hay that had stuck to her dress, and walked towards the men. As she approached them, one by one they stopped talking and nudged each other until finally there was silence. The children, sensing something was wrong, also fell into silence but looked bewildered at the woman who had caused it.

"Good day, mistress Shasta, you be back then?" said one, incurring a dig in the ribs from his companion.

Not understanding his comment, she asked him what he meant.

"Begging pardon, mistress, I be talking out of turn," he said, taking his hat from his head in respect and hoping to be questioned no further.

Confused, Shasta walked away from them towards the forest and May's cottage. What a strange thing to say and where have I supposed to have been she wondered as she walked to the edge of the forest. Picking up a flower that had been broken from its stem she began to straighten the petals and held it to her nose to inhale the perfume. As she walked deeper into the forest, she once again marvelled at nature as it surrounded her. The silence engulfed her. Very rarely were birds heard this deep in the forest. Even the sun struggled to shine through the thickness of the tree branches. This allowed the floor of the forest to remain cool and encouraged the moss to stay moist. Sometimes the sun in Shasta village was exceptionally fierce and the coolness of the forest made a welcome change. Seldom did the gentle night rain penetrate through the trees in this part.

Reaching the edge of the forest, Shasta decided to walk across the village green. As she did so she was aware of startled looks from some folk and smiles of acknowledgement from others.

"You be back safely then, mistress," said one doxey as she left the tavern much the worse for drink.

When Shasta looked at her blankly the woman hurried on.

The quicker I get back to May's cottage the better, she thought.

Hurrying through the rose arbour at the front of the cottage, Shasta saw May engrossed in tidying up the geraniums.

"May," she called out, "hello."

May was so startled to see Shasta she keeled over with shock and lay on the ground getting her breath back.

"Whatever is wrong, May, are you ill?" she asked.

"Mistress, you're back. I have been so worried for your safety." Merlin came back a couple of days ago looking very thin but I have started to fatten him up with some juicy fish," May said as she stood up with Shasta's help.

"What on earth are you talking about, May, and why does everyone keep telling me that I'm back when I haven't been anywhere?"

"Don't you remember how you and Merlin went back in time to try and change the past?"

"I was asleep in the hay field and have just awoken. I keep being told that I'm back. I just don't understand," she said completely confused by now. "Can we go inside and talk, May?"

211

"I think we had better," May said.

Fortunately Shasta's parents had taken a walk into the village and, as they had only just left, wouldn't be back for some time. Entering the cottage she noticed a black cat curled up on the chair in the kitchen. Absentmindedly she stroked him, commenting on the fact he looked at home in the cottage. Merlin, in a deep sleep, jumped and let out a loud meow. Recognising Shasta's scent his eyes flew open and he jumped into her arms, much to her shock and amusement. She only just managed to hold onto him.

"Goodness me, you're a fine cat and what are you called, I wonder?"

"Oh mistress you're back at last," said Merlin with relief licking her face.

Startled by his voice, Shasta dropped him and backed away, her face white with shock. The cat had spoken to her and called her mistress, and yet again she was being told that she was back. Falling into the nearest chair, she asked May what was happening to her. Was she perhaps going mad? Admittedly she couldn't remember what happened before she had fallen asleep by the hayrick, but everyone had lapses of memory at some point.

"Oh, mistress Shasta, can you really not remember anything of what has happened?" she asked.

"No, May. Will you please tell me what's going on?"

Gradually May told her all that had happened from the time she had come to visit her. How she had matured into Shasta and the fact that Merlin had become human again, why they had gone back to the past to try and change the future, and how finally Merlin had appeared at the cottage as a cat once again.

Fortunately her parents weren't here which gave her time to try and make sense of all that May had told her. She decided to go outside to the garden to think over all she had been told, which also gave May time to prepare her explanation for her sister. As she left the cottage, Merlin trotted by her side. He did not intend to leave

212

her again for any reason, whether cat or human. Shasta thought about all she had been told whilst Merlin had curled himself around her in the garden seat, snuggling as close as he possibly could. It was no wonder everyone in the village had remarked about her being back. Slowly her mind allowed her to remember what had happened in the past. She cuddled Merlin closer and tighter, protectively, causing him to meow in discomfort. With tears dripping into the fur of his coat, she said, "I'm sorry, Merlin. I'm just so pleased that you survived. I'll always love you, whatever happens."

"Thank you, Shasta, and I'll always love you too," he said.

Merlin raised his head and brushed it lovingly against her face. As she rubbed gently behind his ears, he snuggled back down on her lap again with a deep sigh. If this was the closest he could come again to heaven, then so be it. At least he was still alive.

May had made herself a cup of camomile tea whilst she mentally prepared herself for the return of Iris and George from the village. What a shock it was to suddenly see Shasta appear from nowhere. Oh well, she thought, at least they were both back safely and, if truth be known, she didn't mind at all if Merlin had to remain a cat. He was company for her now that Erasmus was not around. In fact she hadn't seen him for several weeks now and no explanation was forthcoming either.

"Hello, May, we're back," said Iris coming though the back door into the kitchen.

George was following her. Sitting at the table they both conjured up a cup of tea. Iris had Earl Grey and George decided on camomile, the same as May. His taste buds had changed since being in Shasta.

"You look preoccupied, May. Are you all right?" George asked.

"I had a bit of a surprise earlier, and if you will put your cup down, Iris, I will tell you both about it." When this was done, May said, "Shasta is back again".

"Shasta! Where? Summer where are you?" said Iris, in her confusion rising and looking around the rooms, eager to see her daughter.

"Before I tell you, I need to explain what has happened to her and Merlin. Shall we go and sit in comfort in the other room?"

Leading the way, May settled herself into her rocking chair whilst Iris sat on the sofa holding George's hand expectantly.

May started at the beginning and finished with Shasta's recent return.

"Oh my poor daughter and poor Merlin," Iris said with what sounded like genuine concern for him. "What an awful thing to have happened, isn't it, George?"

"At least she's back safely," he said quietly and put a protective arm around his wife.

"Yes, they're both back safely at least, but where are they?" Iris wondered out loud.

"They're in the garden taking everything in and coming to terms with it all," said May. "Can you bear to give them a little bit more time, Iris, before seeing them?" asked May. The look on Iris's face answered her. "Very well, I will go and tell her you have returned. She must be just as eager to see you both."

Telling Shasta that her parents were back and waiting to see her, May saw a look of hesitation on Shasta's face.

"Come, mistress, it will be alright. They are so eager to see you and are aware of all the changes you have gone through since you came to Shasta."

Shasta put Merlin onto one of the cushions she had been laying on and, with some trepidation, stood up. Slowly she made her way up the garden and turned and waited for May, feeling excited at seeing her parents again but at the same time nervous. May, sensing this, put a comforting arm around her and together they made their way towards the cottage and Shasta's parents.

Walking into the kitchen, Shasta looked at the back of both her parents who were seated at the table. They didn't look any different at all and yet she had expected them to. So much had happened to

214

her since they had left her here as an eight and three quarter year old girl. She had lived another lifetime and known true love. Without realising she had done it, Shasta sighed deeply, which caused her mother to turn around.

Iris took in the beautiful young woman standing in front of her and was at a loss for words. Could this really be her daughter, Summer, the long blonde hair in a plait similar to May's, the gold and silver bracelets adorning her arms but, more than anything else, looking wise beyond her years and her eyes expressing such tragedy? She held her arms out to her daughter in anticipation. Shasta, hesitant at first, then ran to her and held on fiercely, reluctant to let go. George watching this could never believe that this was his young daughter. He had imagined the changes from the description that May had given him, but she was far more beautiful than he had expected. Standing up, he pulled his wife and daughter apart so that he could hug her. Finally releasing her, he was aware that his face was wet with tears, as were Shasta's and Iris'. May looked on with joy knowing that everything would be all right. Merlin becoming human again was unlikely, but at least he was alive. Having given her parents her own version of what had happened to her and Merlin, Shasta suggested they celebrate with a fine meal where Merlin was to join them. May and Shasta couldn't wait to see George and Iris' face when they heard Merlin talking to them. Shasta went out to tell Merlin the good news but he had gone. She didn't have to look far. He had wandered away to the edge of the forest.

"What are you doing here, Merlin?" she asked when she eventually found him.

"I felt a bit left out, Shasta, so I decided to go for a walk," he said sadly.

Picking him up and hugging him to her breast, she carried him back to the cottage, whispering endearments to him all the way.

"Come and meet my parents, Merlin, and, yes, they know that

you can speak, so don't worry."

"Can you see me smiling?" he asked cheekily.

"No, but you look like the cat that has got the cream," she said laughing.

As Shasta carried him into the cottage, she put him on the floor and introduced him to her parents. Obediently he sat down and, for effect, held out his paw as a dog would.

Amused, Iris took his paw in her hand and shook it.

"I'm very pleased to meet you, Iris," he said

"Well whatever next?" said Iris laughing.

Chapter 43

Now that Shasta had returned safely, there really wasn't any reason to stay longer but, by mutual decision, they decided to anyway. Shasta suggested that a fête be held on the village green so that her parents could experience the community spirit of the village in its entirety. It would also be a good opportunity to say goodbye to everyone.

When May went to the village the next afternoon to deliver the potions prepared by her and Iris, she approached the villagers to tell them Shasta's idea. Everyone had heard that Shasta was back, also that she had been unable to change history after all. Merlin had remained a cat.

"Let's do it this weekend," said one villager.

"If we all work together we could make it very special for the mistress," said another.

Leaving them to make arrangements, May walked back to her cottage humming quietly to herself. *Maybe Erasmus will come as well*, she thought to herself. Oh well, she would just have to wait and see. She certainly wouldn't raise her hopes. He hadn't been around for some time now. At least she still had the book.

On the Friday before the fête, Shasta wandered down to the village with Merlin at her heels. She was deliberately walking slowly to enable him to accompany her at a sedate pace so that she could hold a conversation with him.

As they approached the green the usual respect was shown to her by everyone she met. The men tugged their forelocks while the maidens bobbed in a curtsey. Each gave Merlin a look of sympathy, and some bent down to give him a pat on his head, for which he gave a meow of thanks. They knew he could talk, of course, but respected the fact that he didn't.

Shasta sat down on the green with Merlin on her lap. As she

gently stroked him, she remarked how festive everything looked, very similar to the last time they had celebrated before they left to go back in time.

Merlin had been pondering on this as Shasta stroked his back lovingly.

Reading Merlin's thoughts she said, "I know things didn't work out as we planned, Merlin, but at least we're back in our own time and you're still alive."

Merlin agreed and sighed at great length.

"If only though..." he said sadly.

Shasta hugged him close to her.

"I know, Merlin, I know," she whispered into his fur.

Taking a last look at everything in readiness for the next day, Shasta lifted Merlin off of her lap and stood up. Slowly she made her way back to May's cottage with Merlin walking beside her endeavouring to maintain some dignity in his catlike state.

Unbeknown to them, someone had silently observed them in the distance. To himself he said, "Soon my, Shasta, very soon, your body will be mine. Merlin will never again possess you. On my next life I vow this."

* * *

The following morning Iris, Shasta and May had great fun choosing the clothes they would wear. They produced a whole range of clothes in their sizes, then spent at least a couple of hours trying them all on. Eventually they all agreed to be different. May decided to model herself on her ancestor, accepting recently acquired first hand knowledge from Shasta. Iris decided on an Elizabethan theme, whilst Shasta decided to stick to her present clothes. She had experienced enough of the past lately. George decided to just be himself and enjoy everything on offer when he got there.

When they were ready, they walked down to the village. Due to the heat of the day they decided on a slow stroll. Merlin was staying at the cottage as any form of entertainment on the village green reminded him of when he had had human form. He was resigned to being a cat as long as Shasta still loved him. Sighing deeply he settled down in the chair in the kitchen and slept. Shasta watched her parents with amusement. They were like reborn children laughing at everything from sticky toffee apples being made to the local children chasing a pig for the fun of it.

Seeing a vendor selling wares from a basket hanging around his neck, George meandered over to see what was on offer. Remembering the story May had told of trysts being formed by the giving of ribbons, he decided to buy two, one for Iris and one for May. He hoped that this would make up for Erasmus not being around lately. He opted for a pale green one for Iris to match her dress and a cream one for May to enhance her black hair. Pleased with his purchase he made his way back to the women. Suddenly the hairs on the back of his neck stood on end. He was convinced that there was someone watching him. Turning around, the only person he could see was a man in the distance wearing robes which reminded him of Merlin the wizard in stories of King Arthur and the Round Table. As he thought this, the man seemed to blend in with the crowd and disappear. Although convinced at first that the face looked familiar, he shrugged the thoughts off as imagination. After all this was to be a day of fun. Spotting the women in the distance he made his way towards them. Both May and iris were touched by the gifts and instantly attached them to their hair. At the same time he made flirtatious suggestions which were all taken in the mood of the day. None of them noticed Shasta's sad look which, although only momentary, reflected her memories of the occasion when Merlin had given her a ribbon for her hair which had formed their own love tryst. Determined to enjoy the day, Shasta made them laugh with her own comments and thoughts.

The smell of the roasting pig drew them towards the crowd

waiting eagerly to savour the first cuts of meat and crackling which had begun to spit. Their mouths began to salivate as they imagined the taste. One rather rotund man dressed like Tweedle-Dum could wait no longer and began to slice pieces from the belly of the pig, burning his fingers in the process. This was the signal for everyone to start cutting pieces at random. George entered into the spirit and tore off three large pieces which he had managed to transfer onto forks that May had conjured up. With fat dripping down their chins, they moved on to see what was on offer to wash it down with. As they headed to their right, they noticed a precariously erected awning on long poles buried in the ground. Getting closer they could see beer barrels with taps on the front. Tankards were lined up on a table to enable everyone to help themselves which they did as soon as they got there. Shasta and Iris settled for ginger beer as they were not as keen on the beer.

Sitting down on the grass beside the beer awning, they were joined by some of the local villagers. Mostly they were just happy to make conversation but others mentioned how well their herbal potions, which had been made by Iris, had worked. She blushed happily to think that they had singled her out for praise. From the corner of her eye she could see George looking on with pride. May and Shasta sat quietly listening bemused. Neither of them could believe the change in Iris. Shasta especially was pleased as it made things a lot easier on her that her mother seemed to take everything in her stride nowadays.

As Shasta looked away to the distance, she suddenly felt a cold shudder run through her body. Erasmus had popped into her mind for no reason. It made her feel sick and uneasy. Why on earth had that happened? Could he be here somewhere, she wondered. Not wanting to dampen the happy atmosphere, she kept her thoughts to herself.

"I have just had the same thought. Shall we walk for a while?" said May quietly to Shasta.

"Yes, I'd like that, May."

Explaining to George and iris that they were just going for a wander around, they walked off slowly until they were out of earshot.

Shasta slipped her arm through May's as much for confidence as companionship. She was feeling particularly vulnerable suddenly.

"Why do you think he suddenly came into our thoughts, May?"

"Maybe because I was remembering that we first met at the previous fair we had here. I still miss him, Shasta, and it's strange that he should disappear out of my life with no explanation."

"I agree, but if you had been back in our previous life, maybe you could understand my apprehension, May."

With silent consent they headed towards the fire, not because they were cold - indeed the day was very hot - but just needing the comfort a fire brings. Talking to some of the villagers doing the same thing, Shasta felt the hairs at the back of her neck stand up on end.

She clutched hold of May's arm and said, "He's here, May. I know it. I can feel it." Shasta's grip on May's arm tightened.

May gently loosened it and tucked her arm into her own. "Come child, lets go back," she said.

Iris, noticing Shasta's pale face, asked if she was all right.

"Yes, thank you, mother. Just tired, I think. I'm sure I'll be alright if I just rest here."

George took out the letter he had in his pocket and re-read it. Henney, his manager in Holland, had written to say that the police were baffled by the vandalism to the garden centre. They had followed up all the usual leads but no one had seen anything. The good news was he had received a cheque from the insurance company and they were making a start to put right the damage done.

"Maybe after dinner we could pay a final visit to Abelia," suggested Iris. "I would like to see her before we go."

"Good idea, mother. In fact, why don't we start back now?" said

Shasta rather hurriedly.

The decision was made and they slowly made their way across the green. As they passed their newly formed acquaintances and friends they said their goodbyes and made promises of a return in the future.

Chapter 44

"Hello, Abelia. It's really lovely to see you again. I do so enjoy watching George having to shrink down to an acceptable size to meet you". Iris said this with more amusement than malice.

"Thank you for coming to see me before you leave the village. I will really miss you all. When you visit May, please be sure to renew our acquaintance," Abelia said with feeling.

"Just try and keep us away," said George. "I intend for us to visit Shasta at every opportunity we get."

"Shasta, you wish to ask me something? Shasta?" Abelia had noticed that she was looking into the distance deep within herself.

"I'm sorry, your majesty, what did you ask?"

"You wish to ask me something, Shasta?" said Abelia, repeating herself.

"Yes, I do," said Shasta. "When we were at the fair I felt certain that Erasmus was near, but at no time did he show himself to me."

Before Abelia could respond, George immediately interrupted and told them of his experience of seeing the man dressed similarly to Merlin the Wizard.

"George, you never said anything," said May and Iris almost simultaneously, word for word.

"I didn't want to spoil the lovely day we were having. If I had known that Shasta and May had had similar experiences, we could have discussed them."

"Yes, I've been watching him," said Abelia. He's biding his time and kicking his heels. He, of course, was the person responsible for wrecking your garden centre, George." Seeing his startled face, Abelia went on to explain why Erasmus had done it. "He needed to get Summer, as she was then, to Shasta. The only way she would come to stay with May would be if you had to leave the country. Iris wouldn't really trust anyone else to look after her, no matter what

223

denials she makes."

Iris gave May a loving sisterly look which didn't go unnoticed by the others. They were aware of the derogatory remarks that Iris had made in the past but that had now been long forgotten.

"Let's not forget that he loves to manipulate people and play with their thoughts," went on Abelia. "So that was why caused havoc at you garden centre in Holland. The police never found any vandals because there weren't any as such. Erasmus was doing it all from a distance. Once Shasta was here, he began to manipulate her into whatever he wanted, including sending her and Merlin back into the past. He was determined to get rid of Merlin so that he could have Shasta to himself. To a certain extent he succeeded. He managed to kill Merlin when he took over Seth's body, but he hadn't expected Shasta's love to be as strong as it was. After all, she is still in love with him even though he's reverted to being a cat, and who knows one day maybe..." Abelia let her words trail off.

"Oh, Abelia, do you really think it will be possible for Merlin to become human again?" asked Shasta.

Even Iris and George leant forward expectantly.

"We shall see, my dear, we shall see."

Shasta felt light-hearted at hearing this. Deep down she had the feeling that this could happen but to hear it confirmed by Abelia made her feel more confident about it.

"I don't think any of you will have any further trouble from Erasmus once you leave here. He knows that he has lost, Shasta."

Abelia secretly hoped that she was right. She didn't want to admit it but Erasmus had regained the strength in his powers and he had ensured that she wasn't aware of many things that had happened. *Maybe I am just getting old*, she thought. Amused by this, she allowed herself a small laugh, which sounded like wind chimes gently disturbed by the breeze on a summer's day.

Saying a final goodbye to Abelia, they returned to May's garden and their own size once more.

They put off packing their cases until the next morning and spent one last evening together, Merlin sat on Shasta's lap making the most of it before she left.

He was to stay with May on Shasta's insistence. It was the hardest decision that she would probably ever have to make, but she accepted the fact that fate had decreed that he live with May while he was a cat. They could always be together when she made her many intended visits to May and, after all, absence makes the heart grow fonder, so it is said.

Chapter 45

George woke up first next morning, reluctant to move as Iris was wrapped around him. He wondered if she would go back to her former self when they arrived home. He hoped not as she had become so much more loving of late and he was enjoying it. Oh well, he would just work on it if not.

As he moved Iris opened her eyes and smiled at him. "Good morning, George. What a wonderful morning," she said, glancing out of the windows. Last night they had left the curtains open while they had watched the moonlight. "When you pack the cases, George, can you pack us some of this wonderful sunshine too? That is certainly something that I will miss."

"Certainly, I will. Now move out of that bed," and he smacked her playfully through the bed covers.

Stretching languidly, she got up, pulled her dressing gown on and went in search of a drink.

Shasta was sitting in the kitchen with Merlin on her lap, making the most of him before it was time to go.

Raising her head as her mother entered, they exchanged good mornings.

"Good morning to you also, Merlin," said Iris, unsure really of what else to say.

It was going to be very difficult for Shasta to leave him behind but she admired her daughter for it.

Eventually they were ready to leave and their cases had been put in the boot of the car. As usual with holidays, they seemed to be leaving with far more than they came with. Using a final walk in the garden as an excuse, George and Iris left Shasta to say goodbye to Merlin. May walked with them, stating that she really had enjoyed their company and was eager for them to return as soon as it was possible. Meanwhile Shasta and Merlin were in a caravan on the verge outside the cottage. May had acquired it recently to try to help Shasta and Merlin recapture some of the past.

"I will miss you so much, Merlin, but I promise I will phone May to see how you are. Perhaps she can hold the phone for you so that we can talk."

Merlin could hardly speak. So much had happened to them both and now he had gone full circle by becoming a cat once more.

"Oh Shasta, life is so hard sometimes. Just when we thought everything would be right, suddenly everything goes wrong. I would give anything to be human again, even for just a moment so that I could hold you in my arms again."

"Merlin, please don't torment us. It makes me feel so sad. I promise that I will come back as often as possible to see you." With this she kissed him on his wet nose and hugged him to her, not wanting to let go.

Finally the time had come to go and, looking through the back window of the car, Shasta blew kisses to Merlin who was in May's arms. He twitched his tail agitatedly.

"There, Merlin, it will be alright, I promise. They will be back again before you know it. You can have a nice piece of fish for tea tonight." May was unsure really what to say to pacify him.

With that she walked up the path talking to the flowers as she went.

Chapter 46

As they reached the top of the hill on the outskirts of Shasta, George stopped the car to enable them to look back at the village and the surrounding area.

With the sun in front of them shining through the windows of the car, it made them feel very lazy and sleepy. By the time they had finally left it was nearer to lunchtime, so May had insisted that they make up a picnic for themselves. No longer would they be able to wish for things now that they were out of Shasta. *Welcome to the real world*, thought George.

Iris said she would prefer to eat outside of the car so, using the car rug to put their food on, they tucked into chicken and salad, washed down with iced tea which they had taken to drinking recently. They decided to stay awhile after they had eaten and just laze in the sun.

Eventually Iris and George began to doze. Shasta sat up hugging her knees and thought about what the future held for her. She had left her home as a young girl of eight and three quarters and here she was now a young woman. What would her friends make of it, she wondered. She certainly wouldn't be going back to school any more, but how she would cope was another matter. Maybe she should have stayed in Shasta with May. It was her heritage after all. She pushed up the sleeves of her dress which had begun to annoy her by hanging over her hands and, feeling weary, she lay back on the grass and offered herself up to the warmth of the sun.

Her eyes began to feel heavy and she closed them.

She was woken by her mothers' scream. Startled, she couldn't think where she was for the minute. As she sat up, the sleeves of her dress covered her hands again and the top of the dress slid over her shoulders. Her mother was clutching her father's arm and looking at her wildly.

"My God, George, what's happening? She's shrinking before our eyes."

Shasta felt nothing at all, except she was suddenly aware that she was reverting back to her old self. The first thought in her head was *I will have to go back to school*.

Full of concern, her parents both tried to cuddle her at once.

"Do you feel alright, darling?" asked her mother worriedly.

"I think so, Mummy," said Shasta immediately returning to being a little girl once again.

"Are you sure?" asked her father yet to be convinced and suddenly realising he had his little girl back again.

"Yes, Daddy. Please don't fuss. I'm fine."

"Obviously the spell of Shasta is broken once you leave the village, so it looks like we have our little tom boy back again, then," George said, secretly pleased.

Iris, unable to take it all in instantly, went to the cases to see if there was anything suitable in Summer's case for her to put on. How strange - she had instantly reverted back to her daughter's given name again. Luckily she found some shorts and a tee shirt in the boot of the car for her to change into. They were a bit grubby but would do until she got home. "Sit in the car and put this on, sweetheart, while we pack up the remains of the picnic things."

While she was getting changed, Summer (for she thought of herself as 'Summer' once again), started to think about what had happened. She wasn't sure if she was pleased or not, and would she change back into Shasta on their next visit to Auntie May? Oh well, she had the rest of the journey to get used to the idea.

The journey passed rather quietly, her parents quietly discussing all that had happened since they had left. By mutual decision it was agreed that nothing would be said of the magical village of Shasta. Besides, would anyone believe them? Even Summer was having difficulty remembering all that had happened.

"Can I go and see my friend Holly when we get back, Mum?"

"Providing it isn't too late, darling. You will have to get used to going to bed early again," said her mother, still trying to get used to her young daughter. *The resilience of children*, she thought.

When they arrived back, the first thing they noticed was a sold sign in the garden of the house next door. They knew it would be going up for sale, and property around them was very sort after, but even so this appeared to be a very quick sale.

Whilst George unloaded the boot of the car and carried in the cases, Iris opened the front door and walked into each room, opening the windows to allow some fresh air in. Then she walked out to the back garden. Firm in her resolve, she sought out Giles, her gardener, to explain what she wanted done. The uniformity of the flowerbeds began to grate on her instantly.

Giles had been expecting her and was trying to hide behind the willow tree. He wasn't in the mood for her Ladyship today. He wanted to get home for a nice cup of tea and a smoke on his pipe, which wasn't allowed here.

"Where are you, Giles. We're back and I'm making tea. Would you like some?" called out Iris.

Giles was so shocked he showed himself.

"Ah there you are, Giles. Would you like a nice cup of tea?"

"Yes, please, Mrs Backer." He was completely thrown by her pleasant attitude. He knew where he was when she was laying the law down to him, usually about a weed he had missed.

"Tomorrow I want to make some changes to the garden, Giles."

Inwardly he groaned, What did the old dragon want now, he wondered.

"In Shasta, where my sister lives, there is no uniformity of flowerbeds at all. Everything just grows together in cottage garden style and that's what I would like here. I know you have spent endless hours getting it to look as perfect as it does, and I also know that you dislike it intensely. Therefore I will leave it entirely up to you how you do it. I do want variety, though, with lots of highly scented flowers. You can also change the shape of some of the flowerbeds, if you like. When you have finished your tea, you can go early. It will give you an opportunity to think about what you would like to do."

Leaving Giles in the kitchen speechless with his tea untouched, she made her way upstairs to unpack the cases.

Giles was still standing there when George came in for his cup of tea. Seeing the look of shock on Giles' face, he said with a grin, "Iris has told you, then?"

"Are you sure that's your wife, George?" he asked jokingly. They had a relaxed informality when Iris wasn't around.

"Oh definitely, but I agree the change in her since visiting her sister is amazing. I think you will find her much more accommodating with the garden in future."

"I look forward to that, then. I'm off home to redesign the borders. Can I really please myself?" he asked, still a bit uncertain.

"You have a free hand by the sound of it, Giles, so treat it as if it was your own."

Unable to believe the change of events, he walked up the road to his own house, whistling. Then realised in his excitement he had left his bike behind. Well, he thought it's not far to walk and it will be quite safe in the shed.

Arriving home without his bike, his wife who did cleaning for Iris occasionally when she was arranging a dinner party, rushed out to meet him.

"Where is your bike? Are you alright? What has Lady Muck done now? She can't have been back more than an hour."

He allowed her to finish and, when she paused for breath, turned her round and guided her back into the house.

"You will never believe what she wants in the garden now, and I have got a free hand to do it. Let's open that bottle of wine and we'll celebrate." By the time he had finished relating all that had happened, they were part way through the bottle. They decided to finish the rest on the small patio in the garden which only just accommodated a small garden table and two chairs. They sat with a drawing pad full of ideas grown out of their years together, but unfulfilled because of lack of space. Giles' wife looked at her husband lovingly; at last he could have the design of garden he wanted, albeit on someone else's property.

It was no wonder he was so excited, especially when he could take his pick of a garden centre at no cost to himself.

Chapter 47

The Backers settled back to life in their home, adjusting with difficulty sometimes as food had to be cooked and drinks did not make themselves, as in Shasta. They had only been away a month but it had seemed twice as long.

George had reassured himself with a phone call to Henney that the garden centre in Holland was getting back to normal.

Iris had been as good as her word and left Giles to redesign everything to his own tastes, sometimes seeking approval if he felt it was necessary. Unlike Shasta, in this garden the weeding still had to be done but Iris left that to Giles, content in seeing the garden as she wanted it. The late summer, flowers were now coming into bloom and she was enjoying the pleasure of cutting them and filling up her trug for arrangements in the house.

Summer and her friend Holly were lying on the grass under the willow tree enjoying their favourite pastime, taking a word and making as many other words as possible from it. They used flower names which were often long and challenging, or people's unusual names.

The family had made an unspoken pact to keep the secrets of Shasta exactly that. Iris was proud of her daughter and the way she had taken everything in her stride. Once again she marvelled at the resilience of children.

During a phone call to May, Iris explained what had happened to Shasta who was now 'Summer' again and May didn't seem at all surprised. Merlin had become very restless, though, since Shasta had gone from the village, but Iris decided it was probably better not to say anything to Summer.

The new neighbours had moved in next door and, as far as Iris could make out, there was only a man at the moment. Iris had seen him at the front of their property.

It was on this afternoon, as Summer and Holly lay on the lawn with their notebooks, that the new neighbour decided to visit. Iris, going to the door, was pleasantly surprised to find a very good-looking man standing there.

"I felt it was about time I introduced myself," said the man. "My name is Sam Sure."

"I'm very pleased to meet you. Please come in. My name is Iris Backer. I was just about to take a drink out to my husband and daughter. Perhaps you would like to join us."

"That would be very pleasant," Sam said.

As he looked at her, Iris seemed to be drawn at once to his dark brown, almost hypnotic, eyes. Indicating that he should follow her, she led Sam through to the garden.

She made the introductions to George and hurried back inside to collect the drinks. This Sam Sure was certainly a good looking man.

Iris put the drinks on the tray and carried them outside. She had made iced tea for her, beers for the men, and iced lemonade for the children.

George and Sam were sitting at the table.

"Children, come and get your drinks," called Iris.

Summer rushed over, thirsty as always, and took the one nearest to her.

"Hello, my name is Summer, and we're playing our word game."

Interested, Sam asked her how it was played. Summer explained it to him in great detail.

"I think Mr Sure has got the idea, Summer. Why not take Holly's drink back with yours?" Iris said.

"What a beautiful child Summer is, Iris." Sam finished his drink, thanked Iris and made his excuses to leave.

* * *

Later on that evening, when Summer was in bed and George was

234

loading the dishwasher, Iris was quietly tidying up Summer's bedroom. On her desk was the notebook she had been using earlier in the garden with Holly.

Curiosity got the better of her, and glancing through some of it, she took it downstairs with her to read later. Iris had started this word game with Summer during the winter months as she was having trouble with her spelling.

"Would you get me a glass of wine please, George?"

"Would you prefer red or white, dear?"

"I think I'll have white, and perhaps some ice to chill it please."

Glancing again at the notebook Iris smiled at some of the words Summer and Holly had come up with. Some were surprisingly complex.

As George was pouring the wine, he heard Iris give a loud groan. He rushed back in, clutching her glass of wine in one hand with the tongs containing an ice cube in the other still poised ready to drop into the wine.

Iris was holding out the notebook to him, her face white and hand shaking. Dropping the ice into the glass of wine followed by the small tongs, he took the book in his spare hand and glanced down. Summer had written two words across the top line and underneath had changed it.

Everything went into slow motion. First, George was aware of Iris going very pale and sliding to the floor. As the glass slipped out of his hand, the contents splattered on the floor.

He looked back at the notebook for confirmation. Summer had written just two words and had changed it into one....

"SAM SURE" had now been changed into ERASMUS. The one word that would change their lives again forever...

Made in the USA
Charleston, SC
24 July 2011